ACKNOWLEDGMENTS

I have previously thanked all the well-wishers and supporters who cheered me on through FORD KNOWS, my Substack newsletter, where this book was first serialized. To all of you I'll say again:

I couldn't have done this without you, and you have my deepest gratitude.

LAMB

TROY FORD

DEDICATION

To Leo, the light of my life

WE REGRET TO INFORM YOU

It must have been around 2004 when I got the note from Wolcott Academy.

"We regret very much to inform you that the family of your classmate, Willam Broeder, has notified us of his passing earlier this year."

The shock implosion of the air in my lungs strangled my cry to a whisper.

"Lamb."

No details, of course, nothing so unseemly from that bastion of WASPness. I tried to call both his parents but their numbers were disconnected. His mom was on her third husband, no idea what her new name was. His father was Dutch, a career diplomat with a whole new family of his own. I read recently on Nederland Wikipedia that he took a post with the European Union around then, so he was probably already out of the country.

For almost twenty years since that terse notice, I've

1

never really known what happened to Lamb, and if our friend Fugie hadn't been lying his ass off a few weeks back, I might never have. Now I'm haunted by the image slowly coming into focus, like finding a box full of twenty-year-old undeveloped film and finally seeing the pictures for the first time.

Just so you know, we called him Lamb, Lamby, Lambchop—whatever the situation called for. He answered to anything, but his real name was Willam, and when we met he called himself Lam—like Liam but no *i*—he pronounced it like they would in Europe probably, like bedlam, flotsam, jetsam, rather than "Mary had a little..."

Something you have to understand about Lamb, though: at six-foot-six and sturdy, he sure didn't look like a little lamb, and you would never call him "cupcake" to his face if you didn't know him. When we were kids he was pretty squishy, running to baby fat, but if there had been a football team at Wolcott the coach would have pounced immediately and run him through the paces. He could have been a real bruiser, but Lamb was soft. Also clumsy, which let him out of lacrosse, and the basketball coach used to shake his head wistfully at the towering sight of him. He didn't do any of the team sports—no killer instinct—and at a place like Wolcott, that was the kiss of death. Even I knew that.

That's why everyone started making jokes about his name. There was another more popular guy named Lam Bo, Chinese-American, and this was around the time of Rambo, wildly popular at an all-boys school. So just Bo became Lambo, haha, he loved that of course, and because some of the guys thought it was funny, Lam became Lam-

B only in part because of his last name. (Overheard on the school shuttle: "Wait, why do we call him Lamby?" "Because he's a huge pussy.")

No one ever laid a hand on Lamb, except the once junior year—he looked like he could break your arm if you weren't careful—but he flinched easy, you know, got all flustered and embarrassed all the time. Placid, slouching, meek, Lamb. He actually did fracture this one kid's wrist— Lamb tripped over his own feet and fell on him, and sure, that kid was pretty rickety, but still.

Anyway, eventually Lamb is just what everyone called him, even some of the teachers who couldn't hear the difference between Lamb and Lam. And later, after Wolcott, I suppose he just adopted it for himself like he was in on the joke, and that was his name from then on.

At one point he got a pretty big tattoo on his back, which looked like a bunch of Japanese clouds or steam from a distance, all black and moody, until you got up close. They were lambs, lambs from behind, little tails, little ears, little eyes poking out. It was super cute, cute like he was cute, you know—not tough. Guys would come up to him and look closer at his tattoo, I guess thinking *Oh yeah, big thug with some sick yakuza tattoo* or whatever, and then they'd see these cute little lamb butts and they'd be, I don't know, disappointed?

One time, we were out at a club dancing with our shirts off and this boy was obviously high as fuck, weird little punk dude getting all freaky on the dance floor trying to grab Lamb's attention and reel him in. Because Lamb was good looking, don't get me wrong, in that big meathead kinda way. And he spoke Dutch which sounds like

German, or at least, not English. I'd be like "Say something in Dutch" and he'd spit out a weather report or something stupid and hilarious, but people must have thought, *Oh, here's a real shitkicker*, this huge nasty punk with the tattoos and the piercings, the mohawk/faux-hawk/green hair/shaved head of the month.

Anyway, we're dancing, and this freaky little guy, he gets around the back of Lamb to look at his tattoo, and I could just see his face fall, turn from mesmerized to disgusted before your eyes. And when Lamb turned around to talk to him—because he said later he did think the guy was cute, even though I could tell he was 100% trouble—once Lamb's looking right at him, the guy pretends to puke—finger down the throat, retching on the floor—you know like "You and your 'cutsie' tattoo disgust me," and then stomps off after putting on that big show.

Lamb was stung, embarrassed, I could tell, he wanted to leave pretty soon after, just grab a bottle and go home. I felt bad for him. I knew it would only have been another disappointing one-night stand anyway, but he always took that kind of thing personally. It happened a lot, he would get all this attention from guys thinking he was an uber-alpha male—*Fuck me into an early grave, Daddy*—until he opened his mouth, and Lamb fell out.

Because he really was a gentle soul, sensitive, even fragile, despite the boots and the big and the scary punk and all that.

But none of this would have come up if Fugie hadn't been lying his ass off a couple weeks ago—that's Refugio, one of Lamb's Berkeley friends that I got to know better when I moved up to the City after college. We were out at dinner with people recently, and Fugie was blah blah blahing about his "stalker" Buck, this lowlife he and Lamb both dated for awhile. I mean, it's been years and years since Lamb died, and I guess no one left but me to contradict anything Fugie says about him—he may not even realize he's lying, it wouldn't surprise me.

As far as I know, the first part was true: Fugie was hanging out with this guy named Buck, not his real name I assume, who the fuck is named Buck? I guess things weren't really going anywhere when Fugie introduced Buck to Lamb and there were fireworks. I wasn't at the club when they first met, but I was at the party when Buck finally asked Fugie, "Are we on or off?" and Fugie said "OFF." Buck went home with Lamb that night, and that was it between Fugie and Buck, the end.

Buck and Lamb went out for a few months—that's another story—and then Buck moved back to Mississippi or Alabama or whatever swamp he crawled out of, and he was dead in a few years—AIDS—so I don't know what Fugie was talking about when he said—lied—that he couldn't get rid of this guy named Buck he went out with way back when, calling him a stalker. I was thinking, *Uh, he seemed more than happy to take the hint and go home with Lamb the minute you finally told him what was what*, but that's Fugie for you.

That same dinner he was bragging about all the schools he got into, how he went and toured Harvard and they offered him a full scholarship, he says, but oh, he just didn't feel comfortable, this brown punk from East L.A. going back East to Harvard. Bullshit! I didn't say anything, but THIRTY YEARS he never told me this story, not once—

and as much as he likes to brag about everything, he definitely would have told me about a full scholarship to Harvard at some point. And why does anyone care now anyway what schools you got into back then? Fuck sake.

The first night we met, Fugie told me he was a "gifted" child. It was summer break, and I came up from USC to visit Lamb at Berkeley. Maybe Fugie liked me, I don't know, maybe he was trying to impress me. We were on our way to a club sitting in my car at a liquor store on University Avenue waiting for Lamb to buy cigarettes.

Fugie gives me this song and dance about how he wasn't just gifted but *psychic* gifted, and this institute in New Mexico had begged his mother to let him go there so they could study him and develop his talent. For fucking real. I have a very good memory, and I am not mistaken: a psychic institute in New Mexico wanted little Refugio Muñoz to come and be one of their baby X-Men. Give me a fucking break.

Needless to say, nothing ever happened between me and Fugie, even though I was into Latin boys (Fugie & Friends called me a Bean Queen) and at the time I dug the whole punk vibe he and Lamb were into. But I knew he was lying then, and I knew he was lying about Buck, because Buck dropped him like a hot potato the minute he met Lamb, and that's why I went back and dug out Lamb's old journals and notebooks and letters, finally. I just couldn't stand the idea of Fugie stealing any of Lamb's truth—even after all these years, it was just too much for me.

And here we are.

POOF

It was 1999, and it had been a little while since I heard from Lamb, but I called and left him a message: I moved to Austin for a minute with a boyfriend, total fiasco, and now I was coming home to SF.

I met Mando—Armando—the one time I went down to SXSW. Hot Latino, good programming job, and he owned his own house just a few blocks from the local branch of my investment firm—by this time, I had my Series 7, CFP, and a stellar client base, so they agreed to transfer me down there. I wouldn't even have to buy a car—living in the City, I never needed one. Mando drove a BMW, and we were together now, right? Wrong.

Turns out, he was an incredibly jealous prick, like wouldn't let me drive his car without him, not even to the store, definitely not out for fun. I don't think I drove more than two or three times the whole year I lived down there, and I didn't make any of my own friends except for a couple of hags who worked in the branch with me. Mando would literally watch my eyes when we were out together to see if I was checking out other guys.

I started looking for an escape, and when I got offered a position as assistant branch manager back in SF, I jumped. But there was the question of where to live when I got back to the City, and then Lamb called me back at work—I could never receive a call from him at Mando's.

He said, *Hey! Just a thought*, I've been away for a bit and I had to move out of my place, but there's this sweet apartment on Guerrero, long-term sublet, friend taking a job somewhere but didn't want to give it up, yada yada, and the rent's a little steep for me but it's got two huge rooms, bedroom and living, and a really big eat-in kitchen/dining for a common area, one-and-3/4 baths, like NICE, and would you be interested in splitting it, you could have the master suite if you don't mind paying a little extra.

He told me the price, exactly half what I'd been thinking so I was like "LAMBCHOP! I'm your boy!" and we were totally excited about living together for the first time since Wolcott days, right? I'd moved up to SF after USC, but we never actually lived together.

You should know, Lamb came from money, his dad's mostly, but his mom and stepdad too, so he got a little allowance every month from both of them deposited directly into his account for years, and it wasn't much but it was enough to cover his rent and keep him fed and the lights on if he was careful, which he usually wasn't. Lamb had his little schemes and side-gigs, and he went to bartending school for real at one point, so he was pretty well set if never swimming in cash.

By this time I was making more money than him because I couldn't just play at a career, my parents weren't sending me an allowance every month going on thirty years old. But Lamb also didn't need to be anywhere 9-to-5, and so I figured this was perfect because he'd be home during the day when I was at work, and he'd be out most of the night when I needed to sleep. I told him no parties, no crazy tricks at all hours, and he was cool with that.

Lamb was not a super outgoing or loudmouth kind of guy, but he did party, even if it was just us hanging out at home, drinking, smoking weed, and playing video games, unless we were dating someone or cruising for a hookup. He got roped into the Casa Loma crowd for a while, this dive bar in the Lower Haight—breeder version of his punk thing, tank girls and pseudo-skinheads—back when he was crushing on this one dude, what was his name? Rama? Not his real name, obviously. He came and went pretty quick, but introduced Lamb to a few people when he first moved from Berkeley to the City. I followed from L.A. and got a job in the margins department at a brokerage firm on Montgomery Street ("Wall Street West.")

Anyway, for fun we were hanging out at Casa Loma, or down at Zeitgeist—rarely the Castro, maybe the Pilsner, or Detour—but Lamb was always painfully shy. While we were all yucking it up, he'd be in a corner smoking and quiet, getting slowly wasted until he was almost falling down, and then someone would eventually work up the nerve to make a play at him by the time he was too wasted to care. They'd go home and have sloppy drunk sex, probably the other guy thinking Lamb was going to fuck his brains out. Lamb being a big old bottom and usually half-blacked out, his tricks didn't get very far—when they got to the part where someone had to get behind the wheel, nobody wanted the job. There wasn't a lot of repeat business.

But talking on the phone with him when we were arranging this new place, he seemed like he was good, like maybe he'd figured some things out—we were all pretty wild and fucked up early on, maybe I would have stuck with the party longer too if I'd had an allowance from mama and papa.

Back in Austin, I moved out of Mando's—I couldn't stay there another minute. I put my little minivan worth of stuff in storage and was couch surfing with my girlfriends for a few weeks while I was working out the details of the move back to California. We arranged to meet with Lamb's friend over at the new apartment and sign a contract on a Saturday around noon, and then we were going to eat and hang out. I flew out Friday night, and I assumed he was working.

The place was gorgeous, a block from Dolores Park, huge bedroom, lots of closet space, white oak parquet floors, crown moldings, clawfoot tub, and guest bath, all redone. His college friend Lindsey had rent control so she wasn't giving it up come hell or high water, but we had to keep a lid on things and not fuck it up. Lindsey was nice, we'd met before but never hung out, and she was instantly delighted I was on the scene as soon as I walked in the door. She told me later how I missed the craziest parts of the last year with Lamb's drinking and, turns out, drug problems.

See, Lamb's *away for a bit* situation? Rehab. Eight weeks, in-patient, paid by his mom of course, but he had been able to get clean, and got his old job back at that bar The Club south of Market. Yeah, we both drank too much in our salad days, and we both had our share of mishaps, but this caught me by surprise—I didn't know he was doing drugs. This was Lamb, Lamby-lambs, best buddy and wingman for years. I guess we all look at our friends through the lens of *me*.

Honestly, it always felt sort of naughty to have a friend that looked like Lamb since I had to clean up and put on a shirt and tie every day. He was always shaving his head, mohawks, crazy colors, leather jackets, bombers, Docs, all that shit. He had piercings—lip, septum, tongue, stretched out ears, nipples, Prince Albert. The few occasions my friends at work met Lamb, they were all a little afraid. He absolutely was NOT a nazi or anything like that, he just liked the style, and he was attracted to that kind of guy.

So I was used to all of that, and at Lindsey's, he was actually dressed down, if anything—t-shirt, jeans, his hair was grown out a bit and just his natural brown, he still had his piercings of course, but he looked almost normal. Lindsey was visibly relieved both by me and with how good Lamb looked, so it was all settled and I thought, *Huh, no big deal, good old Lambchop.*

That Saturday, we paid the deposit, got the keys, and I helped him move his shit over from his old place in my rental car. The old roommates were cool, they were friendly and all, and they let him keep his stuff there while he was in rehab, but it was clear they were glad to be rid of him and actually surprised at how normal I was—seemed to everyone like Lamb was going to be OK.

We grabbed a burger at Sparky's. Lamb was sweeter than sweet, tender, even grateful. "I love you, D" he told me, with that bashful way he couldn't make eye contact, and I was really touched. I flew back to Austin, wrapped things up at work, loaded my stuff in a U-Haul and drove back to San Francisco the next weekend.

But Lamb wasn't there when I arrived. Nowhere to be found. No answer on his cell, and his voicemail box was full. He'd checked out of rehab, and just ... disappeared. His stuff was all in the new apartment exactly where we left it, untouched, but he hadn't slept there, had moved everything in except himself.

I had to schlep all my stuff up two flights of stairs by myself, not that I had a lot, and I started calling around, called Fugie, called Lindsey, a couple other friends, where's Lamb, have you seen Lamb? Nothing.

That was it. I never saw him again.

I finally called his parents before calling the cops, and they said they'd heard from him but didn't have a number. I checked again a couple times over the next few months, he was in New Orleans or he was in Las Vegas depending on which one you asked, but they said they had long since stopped paying for his cell phone, and eventually his allowance too because they figured he went straight from rehab to a drug dealer or an old boyfriend or who knows what, and enough was enough.

Lindsey said if I wanted to get a new roommate that was fine too, but I just decided to stay and pay for it myself, it really was exactly how much I had budgeted, and I even got a raise at work as assistant branch manager so it wasn't a big deal. As a bachelor pad, it was actually the nicest place I ever lived.

But I still had all of Lamb's clothes and video games, his journals and letters, just ... no Lamb.

Poof.

EAU DE LAMB

Was I mad that Lamb skipped out on our apartment? That's what everyone wanted to know after the dust settled and it was clear he wasn't coming back.

I really wasn't. Lindsey stayed in Toronto and ended up getting married, so I sublet that sweet place from her for about seven years. I always figured Lamb would probably move out after a year or two anyway, he never stayed in any given apartment too long.

But honestly, I just missed him, you know? We'd been friends since high school—neither of us stayed in touch with anyone else from Wolcott. Even if we didn't see each other for a while, every so often I'd get a letter or a call and it would be like he was right there with me, no change, more brother than my real one.

A celebrated correspondence he would call it, so goofy—he thought if his writing ever took off, people might want to read all that, and he would always add *P.S. Save this for posterity!* to his letters, so I did, and later I found my letters to him in his stuff, too.

A couple people asked if we had a falling out—or if we were actually getting together as a couple, if that was the reason he just cut contact and disappeared, because he couldn't handle it. That was definitely not it. We fooled around a couple times back at Wolcott, but having to hide that we were gay from everyone just sort of sealed this bond between us. In some ways, it was more intimate than sex—I didn't need a fuck buddy, I had a hand for that. Two!

So no, I wasn't mad, I was worried—something was really wrong, something had shaken loose in him. When I got to SF to meet him and see the place, I was surprised things were so bad he had to go to rehab. I told him I totally supported him, but there was 100% no way it was going to work if he started using again once we moved in together. I had a career, and it wasn't like I was prioritizing that over him, but I had to support myself.

He knew I was a scholarship case at Wolcott, he knew I still had student loans from USC. In the early days, it was Lamb who usually had the money, and I borrowed from him when I needed someone to spot me a couple drinks or get into a club if we couldn't jerk someone off to get on a guest list. But that all reversed once I got some traction at the firm and a couple of promotions.

I guess I always figured he was ashamed it had gone so far, the drugs, and that the pressure of knowing he couldn't let me down when we moved in together was too much. Plenty of people relapse, sometimes the minute they walk out of rehab. As the weeks wore on and it was clear not only that he wasn't moving in, but that he wasn't even coming back for his stuff, I packed it all up in a closet and got on with my life.

He had that funny smell about him, not a bad smell, it was kind of nice actually, like fresh-mown grass—you probably wouldn't even notice if you were just out and about with him, but if you visited his apartment or his room, you noticed it. His dorm room at boarding school had it, I was always like, *Ah yes, that whiff of Eau de Lamb.* Even though he never lived on Guerrero with me, it hung around the whole time in that closet where I stored his clothes and boxes. I'd open the door and get a face full of Lamb, and it was like he was hiding in there or something, sometimes I opened it on purpose just to remember him. Very strange.

I didn't touch his stuff for a long time. After a year or two, I started filling in the corners of the apartment, and I thought I would consolidate some of his boxes and make a little more room in that closet. I didn't read his journals— I still assumed at some point he might be back to pick it all up, ashamed but alive at least. I borrowed some of his clothes, some t-shirts and a jacket I liked, and I went through some of my old letters to him, I figured those were fair game.

Here's one I wrote to Lamb when we were in college, early days, the beginning of our correspondence back in the 80s:

Dear Lamb,

Thanks for your letter + poem + drawing. Your dream house is now on my wall. Enclosing this May Sarton *book* in hopes that you will find it good. I read it by accident (I was drawn to the title) over vacation—your letter reminded me of it.*

[*That book was *Journal of a Solitude*.]

I'm still sort of confused about this one part of your plan: are you seeing yourself alone by choice or by circumstance? Because I feel that being alone can be both a positive and healthy thing and it can also be vastly destructive to your sanity and well-being—you know?—whether it's because you haven't chosen it or whatnot...

[Skipping over nonsense about me, USC, and L.A.]

So what I was saying before about solitude—is it something you want or something you see as the inescapable future? Please understand that I totally don't mean to pry. I just feel the most compelling candor in your letters and in writing to you, something we didn't really have so much out in the open back in school days. And if you want to share your life with somebody there's no reason why you can't...

I think May Sarton has a little insight into it—or a lot. I don't know if I liked this book because it was as it was or because she mentions so many things that I've thought about on my own, and that you think about too it turns out.

Well—take care Lambchop. Write when you can.
—D.

That's the part I've been mulling over all these years since, because Lamb used to talk about wanting to leave everything behind and go buy a couple acres of land far away, maybe something up in Washington or Oregon, and just live, grow his own food, read, write, be free of the trouble he always seemed to have dealing with people.

In some of his letters he talked about living in a camper—at one point he even went to a used RV dealer somewhere in the East Bay to see how much they cost. He thought he could live in something like that while he built a little house for himself, and he wouldn't mind that too much.

I still have that drawing he sent me, it was just one little corner of a cottage, with a stone wall coming off it and flowers, lots of flowers, wild colors, he even labeled them: *hollyhocks, foxglove, nasturtiums, delphiniums, dahlias, sunflowers*—his mom was a gardener, and he had more than a few flower tattoos. *Lamb's Huis* he wrote in the corner, and in a window, peeping out behind the curtain, a cute little lamb. He wasn't a bad artist, actually, I kept it on my wall all through college.

I half-hoped that's what he was doing at first, when he didn't show up: maybe he finally went and bought himself that camper, found a little plot of land up north somewhere, and was just growing corn and potatoes and flowers, keeping to himself. I thought for a long time that maybe after he got settled, I would get a letter like the old days, explaining everything and maybe inviting me to come up and visit. But none of that ever happened.

What did happen was that Fugie was shooting his mouth off at dinner a few weeks ago, and after all this time, I went out to the garage and found Lamb's old boxes. Not that I was going to confront Fugie with the truth—I knew he was full of shit—but also I got curious about what Lamb maybe wasn't telling me.

Anyway, I went through his journals and notebooks. I guess there were a few gaps in those last years he didn't share. When I first opened the boxes again—it's been, what, almost twenty years?—they still had that same waft of fresh cut grass, Eau de Lamb, faint but unmistakable.

Now that the boxes are open and it's all been airing out for a while, the smell is gone.

HOPE GARDENS

Among Lamb's papers, I found a dozen or so handwritten stories, rough drafts mostly. Some were also typed up and looked like they were submitted to magazines, returned in self-addressed envelopes with form rejections, this one with a scrawled note encouraging him to submit to a zine called *Freak Parade* and saying they liked his style but the content was too edgy for them.

In journal entries from 1993, he wrote about punk rocker GG Allin (born Jesus Christ Allin to a fanatic Christian doomsdayer father) and how his death by overdose had been celebrated in a crazed night of partying at Casa Loma in the Lower Haight. Apparently, someone just back from NYC had swiped one of the polaroids taken of GG the night he died, and as it was being passed around, they debated whether he was ODing or already dead in the picture.

That same night, a very drunk girl fixated on Lamb,

friend of a friend, burned him on the arm with her cigarette, stuck her hand down his pants, and then tried to strangle him in a booth while the party raged on around them. She was petite, probably couldn't have strangled a baby chick (he wrote) but when he pushed her away from him finally, she laughed at him, called him a faggot and demanded he slap her which of course he wouldn't. Then she slapped him, and when he didn't react, tried to slap him again, so he grabbed her by the wrist, and then the other one too as she kept at it. All the while she's screaming every nasty thing she can think of, more and more incoherent, and when her friends all started laughing at her—I guess she was well known for this shit—she sat cross-legged on the floor and cried for so long Lamb left the bar, afraid he had unintentionally hurt her.

He made another journal entry a couple years later that he was in Alphabet City in New York, and visited The Gas Station, the punk club at East 2nd and Avenue B where GG performed his last show and then overdosed in an apartment across the street.

Lamb wrote the short story which follows early the next morning on his friend's couch. He had dreamed of GG buried in the grave his father forced him to dig for himself IRL in the basement of their off-grid cabin in the backwoods of New Hampshire—one hole each for GG, his mother, and GG's little brother.

I wonder why the father didn't dig a fourth grave for himself if he planned to make good on the suicide pact he urged on his family?

"Hope Gardens"

Willam Broeder

A burst of flame, a face bright, gone—here, there, near the street, across the street, on the sidewalk, to his left, down front, at the back of the hall.

Chemical reaction. He said this to himself over and over before the show, each time a match struck, a lighter flickered, a cigarette glowed into life.

Chemical reaction. Chemical reaction. Chemical reaction. He was a chemical reaction, they all were, fire was chemistry, also: fluids, powders, potions.

With red blue yellow flashes flying around, he screamed. Faces loomed toward him and away, faces, faces, faces turned toward him, faces yelling.

"GG Allin is God! GG Allin is God! GG Allin is God!"

Shut the fuck up.

All night, through the pinhole of whiskey, the haze and slip, the liquid churn, the scream of the music and his own voice, raw, so raw it cracked, faces flew apart, his face bloody as he shrieked and they punched, and he swiped back at their leers and their howls. Gash, bash, tear, rip—tear it all apart.

"GG Allin is God! GG Allin is God!" That one guy, motherfucking idiot, screaming over and over, wanted his face smashed, wanted his teeth knocked out, watch them skitter across the floor, people stomping them into crumbs with their boots, snorting the crushed up teeth.

He went after that dumbfuck, tried to bash him with his

head but missed, ended up on the floor, took a kick, didn't feel it. He went on stage wearing a black trench and a jockstrap, but the trench was long gone, he wiped the blood from his eyes, his hands covered with blood, people screaming—"GG Allin is God!"—that fucking guy—mayhem not three songs in, the band pulled back behind the stage and left him to it.

Stomp, kick, pound—someone ripped his jock pulling him off some dick that punched him, it broke, now naked but for combat boots, thrashing around, now people laughing and pointing—"GG Allin is God!" *FUCK that FUCKING asshole!*—and he burst out into the street and the crowd followed. Tear this motherfucking city down, trample it and everything in it, into dust, into lines big as an avenue, snort them all up and scream, and he screamed, and everyone screamed and followed him outside.

He marched up and down, scared people passing by. Red and blue and red and blue flashes, fucking pigs squealing, blocking the way to Johnny's place. He hid in the narrow alley full of weeds and trash next door. Still he saw faces and flashes—poof, cigarette, face, darkness, here, there, by ones, by twos—he thought they would never leave.

The alley was his home now.

In the long gloom away from the street, light faded to murk. They would devour him, demons gnashing, tear him to pieces with rusty hooks and broken glass, he didn't care—

(his papa whispering *the end is near* instead of *goodnight I love you*)

—gibbering ghosts, long knives, guns, brain matter—

23

aborted, murdered—melted into darkness, a pile of trash, an overturned shopping cart. He puked from the adrenaline and the crank and the whiskey. He laid his cheek on the cold, licking asphalt.

The noise in the street shifted. At the mouth of the alley, the path to Johnny's door was clear, Johnny who waved at him, *come quick*, he dashed and they laughed and laughed all the way upstairs.

Someone lined up some coke and he snorted it. Someone handed him a whiskey bottle and he gulped it. Someone gave him back Lily's dress (*Lynn? Lily?*) the one she threw at him after they argued, after she slapped him and he punched her in the back, she called him a cocksucker and said *Put this on asshole!* a long black dress, the dress he wore to the club. He crawled back into it. At the party now, she wouldn't talk to him.

He fell downstairs with some guy, down the block and back to score, ripped the dress—a woman saw them coming, stopped, crossed the street—they met some other guy at a building down the way, he didn't want them to know which apartment he lived in, they ran back to Johnny's, nobody had a needle so they snorted it.

"Lynn? No, Lily!" he yelled at some dude. Lynn or Lily? No, Lily was that other chick, the one he went to jail over because he cut her, but she cut him too, but he had a record so he's the one who went to jail. *Bitch.* "Yeah," the dude said, "bitch."

He snorted another line, yelled for them to *TURN OUT THE FUCKING LIGHTS* too bright, in the dark— *FLASH*—they passed a polaroid around, flashes in his face, he punched someone, no, a wall, maybe he broke his hand.

Shots of whiskey. Flashes. A flash was a chemical reaction too.

Two guys cornered him against the wall, FLASH, their red faces headlights, they put a cigarette in his mouth. He puffed, talked about touring Europe, two girls pulled them away, nervous.

He slid down the wall, no need to talk.

What was that yawning damp bed? What was that tumbling over and over?

He started awake, folded on the floor—"LET'S GET THIS PARTY STARTED!"—he snorted up a fat line, all for him, voices, tunnel, trash, broken glass rattling, he felt himself squeezed and then, POP! Chemical reaction.

What was birth but a flame blown into life—what death but that flame snuffed out—

[to his mama first and last *you killed me*]

—murmuring at the dried foam of blood on his lips, hissing at the dried film on his eyes, a scream. *FLASH*

WE

Tall as he was, Lamb's limbs did not fit together especially well at fifteen, a lost cause for almost every sport. Lamb in motion looked like that early silent movie of a horse galloping—more lollop than hustle, like he was catching air. The cross-country coach, Mr. Hanna, could barely contain his irritation that Lamb's legs just would not move faster.

Meanwhile, I had a nasty broken arm from skateboarding over the summer, and had to sit out lacrosse and baseball my first year at Wolcott. I got stuck in intramurals, jogging mostly, weight training and swimming once the cast came off. That's how we first hung out: Mr. Hanna sent Lamb out to run on his own, building his endurance for long-distance events supposedly, but really just abandoning him to jog along with the only intramural conditioning student that autumn, me.

On that first day of the season, we fell in together doing

laps around the old track off at the far side of campus while everyone else trained on the new track. Around we jogged endlessly—we didn't really say anything, not even a nod that meant *together*, it just happened. I was shorter and took two quick strides for every one of Lamb's slow-motion galumphs. We didn't run right beside each other at first, more like two lanes apart, but this narrowed over the next lap as we realized we were pacing ourselves against each other. Come to think of it, Lamb huffing and getting all sweaty next to me was the first time I noticed that faint grassy smell of his. By the third lap, I stopped wondering if my extra-tall shadow would suddenly break ahead or fall behind—I realize now we were already forming what would become an enduring friendship.

I remember it was my first chance to really look around at the vistas surrounding campus. They don't really give you a natural history tour of the Central California Coast when you're applying to Wolcott Academy, it's all about academics and athletics. I guess it's worth painting a picture for you—they didn't call it Wolcott Country Club for nothing.

To the north of the track, a big grove of gray-green eucalyptus traced the far edge of campus, and past that, a canyon with a winding road to the backcountry—state land, scrubby hills—unused except for the occasional run of county vehicles to assess the threat of wildfire, or maneuvering practice with the big engines. Up the other side of the canyon and beyond, deep green avocado orchards and dry chaparral.

Around the bend, mature coastal oaks and school buildings—dorms, classrooms, the auditorium, all Mission-style adobe and cedar shingles—crowded the front western edge of our hill looking toward the Pacific. We were up on top of a high flattened mesa, so there were fantastic views of the ocean from the balconies of all the dorm rooms. We were only about two miles from the beach, but the moisture and cool breezes mostly never made it up to the plateau of the school and Wolcott Ranch.

Down the homestretch, southward, the coast widened into a hazy lowland, and then, strangely, more Pacific owing to the odd jutting geography of the area. Along this inner rim of the Santa Lucia range, ritzy communities perched above the expanse of farmland and pristine views.

A lot of the boys' families lived on estates in these enclaves, as far away from the squalor of Malibu and Beverly Hills as possible—a couple of celebrity kids, though mostly the sorts of names buried deep in Hollywood and Wall Street corporate filings. Some of these legacies—sons of senators, trustees, and Fortune 500 board members who had also gone to Wolcott—would return not too many years after graduation for bougie weddings (think seersucker, straw hats, and flip flops) in the stately Mission Revival chapel perched at the south edge of campus overlooking their elite empire.

And finally, rounding that last bend of the old track, Wolcott Ranch itself, and the original Wolcott family home where the headmaster lived, grandson of the founder, Scot Prentiss Wolcott. The avocado orchards surrounded the borders of school property and swept out, down, and up again over ridges in three directions.

Squarely between school and ranch, from a time when there was a student riding program and the Wolcott family's farm workers still got around on horseback, what was once a shared barn had been converted into teacher housing. The Bachelor Barn had a few decent studios for the newest teachers, overflow mostly—the married ones either had comfortable houses, or larger apartments connected to the dorms.

But I wouldn't find out a lot of this until later. That day, I was just soaking it in.

This was how our conversation went—*me* (chatty new sophomore) and **Lamb**, (second year sophomore) enduring my patter:

What's out past the trees?
Reservoir.
Have you been there?
Freshman hiking trip.
Can you swim in it?
I wouldn't.
What's down there?
Fire road.
What's that?
It's for trucks to get up into the hills if there's a wildfire.
Does anyone use it?
Not that I know of.
Has there ever been a fire?
I don't know.
[More, much more of this—I was always a talker...]
Do you surf?
No.
Good, those surfer boys are pretty full of themselves.

Great tans, though. Nice tan lines.

[No reply.]

Do you ever go down to LA?

Used to, my mom just got married again and moved to Texas.

I go down sometimes with my brother. His first year at USC, we'd go over to Pico and Alvarado, there was this gas station, like a fucking drive through for drugs, you'd pull up and all these Mexicans would come running up to your window and say What you want, chico? *and we'd buy weed, usually, but he bought coke once.*

You've done coke? [That got his attention.]

Yeah, well, just with him, that one time...

There was a pause.

"You ask a lot of questions," Lamb said. That shut me up for a bit.

Back around for another lap, comfortable with our silence and the satisfying crunch of red gravel, eventually I decided to poke him, just to see.

"Dude, you should get a jockstrap."

Lamb would later write in his journal how I nettled him that first day of our friendship—how he was surprised by my fearlessness. ("*He's a wiseass, but not mean like some of them,*" he wrote. "*He was right though, I was flopping around. But why would he even notice?*")

"What the fuck?" he wheezed out, stuttering to a stop and bending over to catch his breath and adjust himself discreetly (I noticed that, too.) I slowed and jogged around him.

"It's cool dude, no one cares—unless you're trying to

show off—big man, big and tall," I teased.

Lamb chuckled at that, rolling his eyes and shaking his head. We started back up and fell into stride—we had about ten more laps to go. We banked around to the bench for water, and then settled in for the long haul. It was still warm in the middle of September, up on the mesa.

As we pounded down the homestretch again, Mr. Perez, the Spanish teacher, swam into view on his way to the barn, giving us the ol' thumbs-up-with-arm-pistons. Perez was barely older than the seniors, just a year out of college himself. The soccer coach had that burnt caramel skin I love, and blond surfer streaks in his hair from a summer in Baja.

"And then there's Mr. Perez," I intoned. The fact that my favorite teacher also took the early surf shuttle down to the beach before classes almost convinced me to overlook the Newport and Laguna surfer clique's cockiness.

"Here's the real question," I said as we waved back and turned the bend, though I snuck a glance back. "Do you think Perez is cut?"

"Cut?"

"Circumcised," I said matter-of-factly. "A lot of Europeans don't circumcise their sons, not like here—all of the pricks in the showers are cut—well, almost all." (I gave him a knowing look, and he blushed, ha!) "Isn't Perez from Spain? He's not Mexican."

Lamb said nothing, suddenly self-conscious about his own uncircumcised wiener, probably. The open showers were a big problem for me—some of the guys wanted it to be social time, chatting and joking around while I just tried to keep my eyes on the tile and get it over as quickly as possible. Still, it was hard not to check out who had the weenies and who had the meat.

"I'll bet he's uncut," I continued. "I wonder how we could find out?"

"We?" Lamb laughed again in spite of himself, and clumped to a stop. "Dude. What the fuck?" I just shrugged and kept going, and he quickly caught back up. I dropped the subject at that point, but that laugh though, his nervous giggle—I got him, I already knew.

DEATH AND THE BIRD

There was nothing I could do about people calling him Lamb—he had picked it up freshman year, so it was already in effect by the time I started as a sophomore.

It didn't help that he spoke perfect Dutch and French—Lamb's grandfather was Dutch, his grandmother was French Belgian—so even though he had spent most of his childhood in the U.S., summers with his grandparents, and bouncing back and forth between New York and Europe with his diplomat father had produced a non-Republican stink about him that the Aryan youth of Wolcott definitely picked up on. He made it through his freshman year pretty much a loner, this gangling beanpole standing a head above everyone else and spending most of his time in his room or the library.

The thing is, I fucking hate bullies. My brother was a huge dick to me when I was a kid, and we only sort of bonded later on after he left for college and decided corrupting his kid brother with weed and booze on Christmas and summer breaks was funny. It didn't take long for me to get the lay of the land at Wolcott and figure out this big weirdo needed a friend. I could see all the tricks these guys got up to with their posturing and one-upmanship, and I really wasn't too interested in being friends with dudes who would walk into your room and say, "I'm hungry, whaddya got to eat?" and then turn around and loudly declare that you were trying to buy friends with Pop-Tarts.

And here was another thing: freshman year, Lamb fell prey to the school prank that made the rounds whenever a crop of new students arrived.

It went like this: someone, usually a sophomore or junior trying to climb the ranks, would pretend to cultivate a friendship with a kid who seemed like he might be queer. He'd pop around the mark's room a few times, ask him for help with something stupid (in Lamb's case, French homework) and then one night, after lights out—with two or three henchmen in on the gag nearby—the guy would sneak into the noob's room and ask his new "friend" to give him a blowjob, as friends do. It was pretty stupid, usually ending in a riot of laughter, and the mark would end up falling in line with the second-tier jostling for the alpha's approval.

But with Lamb, the gag went sideways. First of all, the guy who tried it on him, Alex, WAS queer, it turned out—years later we ran into him in SF and he was gay as a goose. Also, Alex was never going to be an alpha, and he didn't have a posse backing him up to hear what Lamb actually said to him, so it was all hearsay afterward, with some saying "no way" and others saying "look at the source" meaning Alex was a dipshit and maybe he actually DID want a blowjob, who the hell knows.

The problem was that Lamb, lonely and outcast from day one, had fallen for Alex's friendly overtures, and even though he was too scared to do anything when Alex made the proposal, he told me he was thinking maybe it could have happened later? Anyway, he said *no*, but like an idiot then told Alex about the time he and this other kid jerked each other off at a beach in Spain, and Alex told a couple people before realizing that without the cohort of witnesses, he was implicating himself as much as Lamb.

So. This was the lost cause I adopted on that sunny September day running laps together on the old track. It was pretty loose and casual at first, I didn't know yet about the prank the year before, or the backstory behind "Lamb" and all that. I was dealing with my own shit.

Like I said, early days still, but around Thanksgiving on a Saturday half-day after I just got my cast off, Lamb came into my room all agitated.

"You gotta come," he said, super serious, and I was like "What's going on?" but he wouldn't tell me. "Please." OK, fine.

Campus was pretty much deserted. Most of the guys took the shuttle into town after classes on Saturdays, or went home for the weekend, so we were alone as we headed into the new science building, up to the biology lab.

They went all out with the new labs, all sorts of gadgets and instruments and stuff. There was a whole wall of shelves with freaky things pickled in formaldehyde, bugs and frogs, a cow's heart, even a human fetus. Totally gross and creepy. But Lamb led me into a side room where there was a refrigerator full of samples, and a big metal box sitting on the counter. He opened up the box, and pointed. There were a bunch of little eggs. It was an incubator.

"So? What?"

"They're too dry, the shells are too hard and I don't think they can get out."

"What are they?"

"Baby quails."

And then I see on a paper towel to one side, a shell that's broken open and an itty little chick half hanging out of it, bug-eyed and covered with goo, sort of shivering even though the inside of the incubator was warm.

"What's wrong with it?"

By this time, Lamb starts to go all red in the face and I can see he's freaking out.

"I was supposed to keep the water tray filled up. Mrs. Powell said I could get extra credit if I took care of the incubation and wrote a paper about the reproductive process—California Quail—Callipepla californica—state bird."

"What happened?"

"The tray dried out—it provides humidity in the heat of the incubator or the eggshells dry out and the babies can't peck their way out. This one had a little hole in its shell, but it just wasn't getting through so I tried to help it, and..." By this time, his nose was running and there were tears in his eyes. "It's suffering!"

"That's nature, dude, happens all the time..." I said.

"But it's my fault! I shouldn't have picked at the shell, and now I don't know if it wasn't ready to hatch, if it was just a crack and I helped it out too soon, or ... look at it!

There's something wrong with it."

Well, fuck. By this time, Lamb was dancing around, tears streaming down his face, and honestly, I was more worried about him than the bird.

"Do you want me to put it out of its misery?"

His eyes got wide, but I think that was the reason he came to find me in the first place, and he nodded. He was in full waterworks mode by then, and I figured we better get it over with quick before someone walked in and found him crying in the biology lab. I picked up the quivering, gawping little chick and brought it out into the lab.

"I need something heavy, like a brick or something."

"No!" he almost screamed.

"Well then some scissors—quick snip and—"

That really got him going, he actually started blubbering, but it seemed like that was the way to go only we couldn't find any scissors.

"We could drop it off a balcony," I said, "the impact should be enough to kill it, it's half-dead as it is."

"Should?" he said, doubtful, sniffling.

"How about this—I'll throw it up as high as I can in the air, and then it will have enough momentum on the way down to definitely do the trick. I promise. It will be like the little guy had his chance to fly and be free, and then done."

Lamb nodded, almost hopeful at the prospect of doing right by this baby chick, poor sap. "Let's hurry." So we walked out onto the balcony overlooking the courtyard between the science and math building, all bricked over, and I figured that was as good a place as any.

"Ready?" He whimpered, which I guess meant *yes*. But I couldn't use my throwing arm because I just got the cast off, so I had to use my left and, well, let's just say my aim was a little off. I wanted it to go as close to straight up and back down to hit the bricks, and it did go up in a nice imitation of flight for a second, but then it went screwy, and ended up coming down on the lip of the math building's roof, bounced off, and then down to the bricks.

"No...!" Lamb moaned, and went racing down the stairs. I followed, and when we got down, well, let's just say it was definitely dead. Lamb sat cross legged on the ground next to it and bawled his head off, while I was nervously looking around to see if anyone was coming, but in the end, I just sat down next to him and the dead bird and let him get it all out.

Anyway, we were already friends by then, but that afternoon with the bird? That was when that big dumb crybaby wormed his way into my heart for real.

THE STRANGER

For the first few years I knew him, Lamb always went to his mom's house for Thanksgiving in Houston, and for Christmas, to his dad and new stepmom's house in Bronxville, New York, just down the street from some Kennedy cousin or other apparently. Swank.

His stepmom, Renée, was quite a bit younger than his dad, so you can imagine there was some tension all around—Lamb's own mother called her *that JAP* ("Renée doesn't look Japanese," I said, baffled. "Jewish American Princess," he explained)—but at least at first, Lamb really tried to get along with her. When she got pregnant our freshman year in college, he was super excited about having a baby brother.

Something happened over Christmas sophomore year. He went back East to spend the holidays, and then I got a letter saying he had cut it short and flown back to Berkeley on Christmas day. He was vague about why, and he never went back as far as I know—from then on, he only saw his dad at his grandparents' house in The Hague, or they would sometimes meet up in Aspen for a ski trip, or dinner in San Francisco.

In Lamb's journals, I found a brief entry from "12/26/88 - Caffè Med"—he always made a note of where he was when he wrote in his journal. Caffè Mediterraneum was his favorite on Telegraph Avenue all through college—supposedly the birthplace of the latte, definitely the place in *The Graduate* where Benjamin is sitting when Elaine walks out of Moe's Books across the street and he chases after her in the bus.

Lamb wrote:

"I would never hurt him, I don't know why she acted so crazy. I thought we were bonding. I guess not. I was just trying to have a quiet minute with him, so he would know me—I'm not going to have that many chances to hang out with him, just Christmas mostly, maybe summer break, but I guess that's all ruined now. I think I might never see him again."

Around the same time, he wrote the following story in his journal—in French—I had to translate it with Google. I guess I'm calling it a story, not a poem, but it is strange. A prose poem? Yes.

"L'étranger"

Willam Broeder

A door shuts, she walks upstairs to reassure.
Into the nursery, back down to her book, fallen to
the floor.
"Safe," she says, reads on a page or two.
New mother—no gladness upon her lips, no light
in her heart.
The King away, back for Christmas.
Outside, in the garden, a candle bursts into flame,
stills to an ember, throbs, throbs.
She sets her book aside, draws the curtain.
Safe, she thinks.
Out of sight, out of mind.
She guards the palace, the new prince.
Safe.

The old prince, strange and queer, looks on.
The wind-whipped trees bend and sway.
Moonbeams dance across the glass, frosted by the
pulse of ghostly breath.
A wrinkled apple falls, rolls and knocks into
another, brown cheek, pink cheek.
The parkway roars and groans, a river of lights
fleeing.
He shivers in his coat.

Slowly, gently, shut the door, up the back stairs.

Searching for it still, not in the garden, not in the
spare.
The carpet wrong, bed too short.
The silver lamp casts about.
What is it? The treasure promised.
Where is it? Not in the closet, not in the drawer.

In the nursery, the gurgle of steam—mobile,
moon, stars—a night light.
"Quiet," he whispers.
"Look at you," he murmurs.
Long he looks; long years to come—summers and
winters; sun and snow.
A curled fist, bright eyes, a dimple, a coo.
He rolls the bundle up in his arms, whispers,
"Safe, safe, safe—" and "Long life—" and
"Blessed—"
"Brother—"

No footstep behind him, just sudden fright, her
fury:
"Why are you here?"
"The treasure—"
"Smoke, and ash..."
"We—"
"Damn you..."
He flees south, flees west.
Stars wheel in a strange sky.

NO MAN'S LAND

I had forgotten about this letter until I dug it up recently—
Lamb's acid trip, one of the most epically bad trips I ever
heard of, except maybe those people who jumped off the
roof of Barrington at Cal because they thought they could
fly. Come to think of it, it came right after the Christmas at
his dad's that he cut short, which is probably why I never
really got the whole story about the banishment.

I also forgot what a stupid dick Fugie was to Lamb, or
maybe at the time, like most kids, I just figured no
(permanent) harm, no foul. Lamb survived, and he didn't
stop being friends with Fugie, but I smelled a whiff of
betrayal about him from the get-go.

Still, he didn't force Lamb to take two hits of acid and
go screaming through the streets of Berzerkeley naked.
And it didn't stop Lamb from taking acid many more times
over the years—we had a ton of fun tripping on the dance
floor at Colossus (aka Colostomy,) Pleasuredome, Rave

Called Sharon, Mr. Floppy, The EndUp. Good times, until they weren't.

1/18/89

Caffe Med
Hey D,

Not sure what I want to say about what happened, but we talked so many times about how much we wanted to do acid, so here goes.

Fugie called me Friday night and said he and his straight roommate got some acid and did I want to do it with them? His roommate's girlfriend wasn't going to take any, she'd be sober and look out for us, drive us up to the Berkeley hills and back down, and it was only $5 so perfect time to try it with someone I trust. And it was Friday the 13th! So cool!

What was I expecting? I don't know. I just remember how the guys used to talk about it at Wolcott, how it was amazing and trippy, that time slowed down and everything came alive, all the lights and sounds would be talking to you like they knew you. Remember that time Jeff Hiller was laughing so hard in his room, and we all went in to see what was going on and he just looked at us and laughed even harder? When he finally could talk again he said it was like a big cosmic joke and he finally got it.

Yeah, so all that happened, only not in a good way. Fuck! So basically I'm just going to say if you do it, be careful because I had the worst trip ever.

So Friday night rolls around, and we meet up around 9:00, Fugie and Chris and Emily and me, and Emily drove us up to this field up in the hills, great view of the whole bay all the way to the GG Bridge and SF. I don't know how they found this place, there weren't any houses around, it was just this grassy hillside and we hiked down to a spot a little ways from the road.

Fugie says, "It's old, you should take 2 hits—me and Chris are going to take 4 because it's kinda weak." So we took it and just sat there smoking, and they were talking and stuff but I was a little nervous. After a while I noticed the lights down around the bay started shimmering, like there were suddenly twice as many as there were before and they were sort of rising up into the air. It looked like jewels or something, it was so beautiful and I started feeling like, yes, this is cool, this was what I was hoping for—like I was finding out a big secret—THE BIG SECRET.

But then Fugie and Chris started talking shit to each other, like "Oops, you shouldn't have taken that acid— you know there's no going back, right?" or "How's it feel to be the biggest loser ever?" and I really didn't understand why they were saying that, their voices sounded really weird, and it was like they hated each other or something and I started to get scared, like how well do I really know Fugie? We met freshman year in the dorms, and we partied and stuff, but we weren't best friends or anything and I didn't know Chris or Emily at all.

I said, "What's wrong with you guys?" and all three

of them suddenly whipped around and stared at me. Chris and Fugie started laughing, and they seemed really sinister but they didn't say anything. That's when I felt like I was the one who made a mistake. You know how they say that every so often someone takes acid and they go crazy, that they never come back down again and they put them away for the rest of their life? Well, that's what I started thinking was happening to me, that I was tricked—like it only happened to people who were giant losers, and I was the biggest one of all.

At this point, they all decided they had enough of sitting around on the hill and wanted to go back down to Berkeley—I don't know where we were supposed to be going because getting in the car suddenly felt very wrong. The backseat, the door—it all felt ... chewy? Does that make sense? Like metallic, but spongy at the same time, and as Emily was driving down the windy road from the hills, it felt like we were out of control— and that's when the music started talking to me.

I don't know what we were listening to, but it was like music was invented to swallow me up, and it was honking and squishing and farting at me, and saying things like "You're never coming back, you're really fucked now, loooooserrrrrr..." and that's when I really lost it.

All of a sudden Fugie and Chris are saying, "Are you OK?" And I was like, "No! Music is talking to me! I'm scared!" By this time we were down in some neighborhood over by the Claremont Hotel, and Emily pulls the car over and she and Chris jump out and walk around to the front, they didn't say anything, it was just like: let's get away from him.

So then Fugie says, "OK, be cool, they want me to walk you back to the dorm, they're going to take off," and before you know it, they drive off and we're stuck in the middle of the night on this dark, silent street—I actually didn't know where we were until later—and I was terrified that Fugie was going to leave me too, but also, I knew it was all over, I had fucked up, I was that one-in-a-million fool who takes acid and never comes back.

It was like the Twilight Zone—it was going to be dark night forever, and I was stuck there, wandering the cold streets, and at some point Fugie would sneak away from me like I was infectious or something and then I really was going to be alone forever. I was now one of those filthy, stinking homeless people wandering around and looking like they don't really see what's in front of them but something else, trapped in some strange dark world.

I told Fugie the only way out was for me to kill myself. I thought I had a knife in my hand, I tried to stab myself in the neck but obviously there was nothing there. No Man's Land—I suddenly knew what that meant—that's where I was, forever, I couldn't even kill myself to escape. And when that really sank in, how irrevocably I had fucked myself—not just for the rest of my life, but actually forever, eternity—I thought, well, nothing matters.

I didn't need clothes anymore, so I took them all off, buck naked. It was just a matter of time before Fugie snuck away, he started laughing at me, so I ran off. I saw the dorms and I ran out into the street, I didn't even see the car coming at me because all the lights were dancing around, but they slammed on their breaks just in time I guess. I still sort of bounced off the hood and went skidding across the street on my knees, tore them all up really bad but I didn't even feel it, and then I jumped up and dashed off through the dorms. Fugie was gone, I was lost, and by this time I was getting cold and running out of gas, so I sat down on the ground.

It occurred to me, slowly, that this was just an acid trip, that it wasn't a permanent thing after all—I must have started coming down a bit—and someone called to me from a window, "Hey, dude, bad trip? Stay there." I was still pretty off my head, so when the cops came, I went streaking across a lawn, and they tackled me and put me in handcuffs. They had my clothes—I guess they talked to Fugie at some point, and he had picked up my clothes, so they helped me get back into my pants and shirt and boots.

They drove me down to Highland Hospital in Oakland, strapped me to a gurney in the emergency room, gave me a tetanus shot, and that was it. A few hours later, some psychiatrist came in to ask me some questions because I had threatened to kill myself (Fugie told them.) I said that was just because I was tripping my ass off. They gave me bus fare back to Berkeley (Fugie kept my wallet so I wouldn't lose it) and I got back to my dorm just as the sun came up. I took a shower and cleaned up my knees, some really bad road rash, and just hid under the covers all Saturday.

Fugie came by later that afternoon to check on me, he said they were really freaked out about what happened. I asked him why he didn't talk me down, when I was saying I was stuck forever, why he didn't explain to me it was just an acid trip and it would end, and he said he started to believe the things I was saying, that he was afraid I was right and he was going to be stuck like me. So much for taking acid with someone you trust. You should see the scabs on my knees, totally gross!

Anyway, I guess I just wanted to tell you to be super careful if you do acid at some point. Do it with someone you really trust, like, not a Fugie.

Lamb

P.S. Save this for posterity!

BURNING MAN

I want to say that something sort of shifted in Lamb after he went up to Burning Man in 1994. I got the story afterward, of course, but I could tell the experience affected him more than he let on. I asked him what's the big deal, why did he care so much what the people he hung out with up there thought? He didn't really have an answer, and got all embarrassed and shamefaced.

I found this in his journal:

"I'm just lonely, honestly. D isn't always around, I mean, often enough to be my best friend and all that, but I'm on my own a lot on the weekends, and I can't rely on just one friend. So I guess I was just hoping to make some new ones where I didn't have to start from scratch, just plug in—maybe that's cynical, not getting to know people but just sliding into their lives without the work of getting to know them—but ... well I just

*find it really hard. People are always wanting
something from me that I don't have. I just want it to
be easy, for once in my life.
So please, please, please, let me, let me, let me,
Let me get what I want this time... haha"*
[That's a line from The Smiths, obv—ugh, he loved
them. Fucking Morrissey.]

This was about a year or so after we both moved to the City.
Lamb moved first, summer of 1993—it was a shorter hop
for him from the East Bay to SF than for me coming up
from SoCal. But even after a year, he still hadn't made any
real connections in the City, and like he said, I was working
weekends so I wasn't much of a wingman for the first
couple of years.

He started temping downtown, and moved into a flat
with three guys down in the Mission on South Van Ness.
For whatever reason he wasn't getting along with them.
There was a vibe almost from the beginning, he told me—
he thought one or two of them might have voted to let him
move in because they thought he was cute and wanted to
date him.

One guy was in a relationship, and one afternoon the
boyfriend started sniffing around Lamb when the
roommate wasn't there, even invited himself into Lamb's
room asking if he wanted to smoke some weed, and
although nothing happened, the roommate got wind of it
and things got more tense if not outright hostile. Lamb
moved into a studio on Valencia by himself pretty quick
after that, and didn't stay in touch with any of them, so
there was that opportunity wasted—roommates are usually

a good way to meet people in a new town.

Anyway, it's clear Lamb was hoping to make some friends at Burning Man. Lindsey—his friend from Cal that I sublet from later on—she was the one who mentioned it. She worked with this guy named George, and he had a boyfriend and a bunch of gay friends who were all going up to Burning Man, she should come, yada yada. What's Burning Man? Big party in the desert up north past Reno, anything goes: clothing optional, drugs, music, drag, whatever you want, get your freak on. I had to work so I couldn't go.

Lamb got super excited—not even so much about the craziness of it but the fact that there was this ready-made group of gay guys that he was going to meet through Lindsey's friend. "This is it!" he wrote in his journal. "I've been waiting so long for SF to split open for me—finally a pinata!!" So, Burning Man was supposed to be his chance to meet some new people, have some fun, maybe find a boyfriend.

They drove all night after work on a Friday—Lindsey couldn't pick him up until almost 9 p.m., it's a seven or eight hour drive from SF, and they stopped in Reno to eat—by the time they arrived early Saturday morning and found where George and his friends were camped, they had been up for 24 hours.

Meanwhile, George and his boyfriend were hunkered down in their tent because they had taken opium the night before and got so sick they couldn't move—some of the BM marshals even came by to check on them and see if they needed medical attention. By the time Lindsey and Lamb got their tent up and unpacked a few things from her car, they were ready to collapse, and just at that moment, the whole rest of the group of friends decided they wanted to go to the hot springs for a morning bath. I guess there were these natural mineral springs on the edge of the playa—that's what they called the big dried up lake bed the whole thing was staged on. ("Like landing on the moon," he wrote, "only flatter.")

Up toddles the cutest cherub of a boy, all bright-eyed and bushy-tailed, and says to Lamb before any other introductions, "Hey big boy, I'm Nathan—wanna go to the hot springs with us?"

But that, apparently, was when Lamb made his fatal mistake, or at least he thought so, like he flubbed the first line of his audition—dismissed and never given another chance. Lamb said no.

"We were driving all night! I was so fucking tired. I had to take a nap. Fucking STUPID! None of that mattered—that NO was poison. He changed right before my eyes from adorable-open-bright to shocked-irritated-cold."

He found out from Lindsey later that Nathan was the humpy party bottom of the group, the bait for the inner circle. Blond, very cute—several of the friends had first been introduced to the group by way of meeting and fucking Nathan. Their little boy tribe was on the prowl for new tops, and if Nathan gave the thumbs up, an invitation to join the group was extended. Not that Lamb would have passed the test. The real audition with Nathan would probably have been just another don't call us, we'll call you.

But for a month afterward, he berated himself for not sucking it up, for not saying yes when he had the chance.

"Dammit! The correct answer was Yes, yes, yes!—let's go to the hot springs together, let's be playful puppies all of us, let's frolic and fuck and be friends and lovers forever and ever."

Apparently, for the rest of the weekend, Nathan wouldn't even look at him, much less talk to him, and neither would any of the other guys in the group except for George once he recovered from the opium overdose later that day, and Stan the old dorm mate, because they were both already friends with Lindsey.

Even when he did ecstasy that first night, and offered the extra hit Lindsey didn't want to Stan, and tried to be friendly and flirty with Nathan, and with Gabriel, the other hot new recruit everyone was panting after—"I caught him looking at me but he looked away when I tried to make eye contact"—that first impression had been ruined and he was officially invisible.

There's a picture of Lamb, only one actually, from that whole trip. Lindsey dragged him out for another visit with the gang to the hot springs. I think she's the one who took the picture.

There's the group in the background—he knew all their names, wrote them on the back of the picture, and a couple of them stand out from his journals—off a little ways, chatting, laughing, painting each other's backs and faces with the mud from the springs. And then there's Lamb, in the foreground, and he just looks so ... isolated? Removed? Apart, anyway, not one of them. Hard to tell what he was feeling, looking off at the horizon, Wayfarers on—nearby, but miles away.

It just seems so Lamb to me, this picture, like the moment that strange sort of resignation took him over after that.

Had he not been so disappointed, Lamb probably wouldn't have been such easy prey for the character that loomed large out of the rave later that night: Count Crunchula.

About a year or so later, Lamb told me that Lindsey caught him up on the Burning Man guys: George had always felt pressured to have sex with all of them, and broke up with the boyfriend, who was verbally abusive toward him. Gabriel died of an overdose at a New Year's Eve sex party—no one noticed until some dude tried to climb on top of him and realized he wasn't breathing.

Stan got really into leather and uniforms, and wouldn't even acknowledge Lamb the few times we went to Sunday Beer Bust at the Eagle.

And not long before I moved to Austin, me and Lamb were walking by Dolores Park, and all of a sudden he stops dead in his tracks and looks back at this guy who had just passed us. I kinda noticed him because he was one of those young dudes who looks like an old man, his boyish looks ravaged by the early HIV drugs—lipodystrophy had distended his stomach, and his face had that gaunt, wasted, almost skeletal look. It was Nathan.

COUNT CRUNCHULA

I've gone back and forth about sharing this episode because the guy who pounced on Lamb up at Burning Man is sort of famous, and I read an article not too long ago that he's been banned from attending a bunch of tech conferences because he was preying on young guys he was meeting at them. According to the article, he was accused of stalking a teenage boy way back in the 70s, so this shit was going on for almost fifty years.

"Count Crunchula" was famous from the early days of hacking for discovering that a toy from a cereal box would unlock unlimited long-distance calling, and he spent some time in jail for hacking back in the 70s. Apparently, he was friends with the Apple guys, Jobs and Wozniak, in the early days, and when we met him, he was a well-known nut constantly doing acid and showing up at raves and underground parties.

Lamb said there was a rave camp set up on the playa

about a mile away from the main Burning Man area because they were blasting techno at all hours and some people actually did want to get some sleep. Lindsey ended up not doing any of the drugs Lamb had brought for them, which was fine, but she was already asleep in their tent by midnight, the night they burned The Man. That meant he was doing mushrooms for the first time by himself (better than doing them with Fugie, I guess?)

At some point he thought that he was turning night into day and back again by blinking his eyes, so he took ecstasy to smooth himself out—an MX Missile, we used to call that. Seems like it worked because he didn't freak out, but he had no way to get to the rave camp to go dancing. It was generally considered a bad idea to walk in the dark with all the drunks driving around off-road. Finally Stan, Lindsey's friend from the dorms, let him hitch a ride after Lamb offered him the hit of *E* that Lindsey didn't want.

There weren't even that many people out at the rave, he said, maybe twenty or thirty, but all of a sudden this weird old guy came bouncing up and Stan somehow either knew or knew of him, and—I suspect to get rid of him—said to Lamb, "This is Count Crunchula, he's a famous hacker, he does energy and bodywork," and promptly disappeared. Of course, Lamb was high as a kite, and when the Count asked him if any "areas" needed work, a very horny, lonely Lamb said, "Yes! Sex!" Oops.

"You fucked him!" I accused him when he told me the story after they got back, but Lamb said *no*. He said he thought the guy was going to do some sort of Reiki and release all his pent-up frustration over not having a boyfriend and all his bad luck at the bars, but they didn't have sex. Still, Count Crunchula glommed onto Lamb for the rest of that night and next morning—no sleep for Lamb on his MX, or the Count on his acid. They made arrangements to get together and do some of this "bodywork" he was known for the next weekend.

To say the Count was crunchy is an understatement. He was about 50 at the time, total acid head, wild salt-and-pepper hair and scraggly beard, and to top it all off, he was missing his front two teeth. The only reason I didn't take a giant step backward when I met him the following weekend was because Lamb seemed to like him—he was the only "friend" he ended up making at Burning Man, and the guy was pretty plugged into this sort of next-level underground scene that seemed really cool to us for a minute.

This is how it went: The next Saturday, the Count picked Lamb up in his old beater car, still completely caked in the dust from the playa that covered everything and everyone that goes to Burning Man. They drove up to Mill Valley and this funky basement studio he was staying in, and the bodywork consisted of the Count literally climbing on Lamb's back, arms and legs wrapped around him like a monkey, and Lamb doing squats and pushups with this creepy dude climbing all over him. There was some poking and prodding too, some leg massaging and other shit, and Lamb was completely oblivious to what was really going on, because, as he said, "It really was a good workout! I was so sore the next day!" Jesus help me—Lamb was such a dummy. Apparently this was exactly the kind of weirdness the Count was still doing to those young guys at these tech conferences that got him into trouble, only there seems to have been some coercion and erections involved.

Ugh.

Anyway, this went on for awhile—but nothing else, according to Lamb, nothing sexual—and afterwards, the Count got on his computer looking on a web bulletin board, which was sort of all we had back in the day, like chat rooms and Netscape or nothing, and he said there was an underground party called Megatripolis that night, invitation only, you had to have a password or something.

They drove back to the City and Lamb called me to see if I wanted to come, he said he wanted me to meet the Count, and there was this cool party at some warehouse in the Mission, etc etc, and he still had two hits of ecstasy. When I got to his place, I was immediately like, *whoa*— this Count dude is super freaky, but I didn't say anything at the time. I gave Lamb some cash for the *E*, to which the Count looked on wistfully, "Nice if you can afford it," and popped what looked to me like about five tabs of acid.

When we got to the party we were already starting to trip. We walked in and these guys at the door looked at me and Lamb and said, "How did you hear about this?" suspicious-like, and we both pointed to the Count and were immediately ushered straight on through, no cover charge or anything, it was not like any club I ever went to.

There was this big, gorgeous blond chick with her hair in cornrows serving drinks on a folding table—Lamb pinched my arm and whispered, "It's Anna Nicole Smith!" and honestly I had to look a little closer but it wasn't her. She served us, and when we asked "How much?" she said in this sexy Southern accent, "No charge, honey, but I accept tips." (Lamb: "Are you sure it's not—?" Me: "Positive.") We each gave her a buck, and she said, "Good luck." I guess it was pretty clear we were already flipping our wigs.

We sat down on the patio for a cigarette and this one guy asks, "What vitamins are you on?" This used to be a standard question at the clubs: Vitamin E (ecstasy) or K (ketamine) or C (crystal meth) etc. We told him we took E and he asks, "How many?" Just one. "Oh. Newbies." And we said, "How many did you take?" Seven! "And I barely feel it anymore..." Well, I never took more than one hit, and after a few times it wasn't having much effect so I gave it up rather than taking more, that shit's expensive!

Then these two kids next to us announced they had taken acid, E, some crystal and smoked a bunch of weed— while sipping cocktails and smoking—and when our eyes bugged out, the girl said, "That's the point, right? Take as many drugs as possible." I don't know how they were still conscious. I asked the girl how old she was because she looked really young. "Fifteen." Her boyfriend was eighteen.

Lamb and I didn't stay too long—I had to work in the morning, we didn't know anyone, the Count was off on the dance floor, and I was already feeling like he was bad news. A fifty-year-old acid head with no job and missing teeth was definitely not a good scene. It should be obvious to everyone by now that Lamb's biggest problem was confidence, and he would make friends with anyone who took a liking to him just because they showed an interest.

We got together a couple weeks later, and I asked him about "the toothless wonder" while we were having burritos at El Toro. "Come on, he's not so bad," Lamb insisted, "I feel kinda sorry for him, you know, I think he used to be somebody in tech or something, but he's got problems." Obviously. "He left me a message a few days ago—I'm hesitating to call him back just because he always wants to climb on top of me and do those exercises." Good grief.

I didn't try to convince him or anything, but when we got back to his place to watch X-Files, I noticed his answering machine was blinking and I just had this feeling it was the Count—who else would leave him a message besides me? While Lamb was in the bathroom, I closed his bedroom door so he wouldn't hear and pushed the button.

"Hey, Lamb, it's me, John—you know, Count Crunchula—I really wish you'd call me back, I mean, I thought we were friends so I'd really like to hear from you. Give me a call."

I deleted the message.

THE WATCH ON THE WALL

I'll never forget the time Lamb dragged me to visit his grandma at some old folks home in Redondo Beach. He came down to SoCal for spring break, I think it was, and on our way to a party in Long Beach, he says, "Let's just stop for a minute—I promise I'll be quick. I haven't seen her in ages and she's really old." So we pull into this nondescript, mid-rise complex right near the beach, and he's screaming into the intercom, "Gramma! It's me, Willam!" and she buzzes us in.

Lamb's mom's family was from LA, and even though her only daughter was off in Houston with her latest husband (some state senator or other—Republican, of course,) Grandma refused to move to a home "in that horrible place" (Texas, that is, or so the legend goes.) Plus, two of her sisters also lived in the same complex. ("Aunt Dolly and Aunt Lolly," Lamb said. "You're shitting me," I said.)

Anyway, it was just as institutional and antiseptic as you would expect: the lobby with the TV lounge set up like a drive-in theater, only wheelchairs; that fake wood paneling in the surprisingly large elevator ("For the coroner's gurneys?" we speculated) and this long-ass, putty-colored corridor to reach Grandma Lamb's front door. The residents were required to flip an indicator switch on their door every morning so the attendants could walk down the halls and scan to see who didn't wake up.

It was like stepping from a grade-school cafeteria into a witch's cave, Grandma's apartment—stuffed to the gills, like she didn't want to part with a mansion full of stuff, and just slotted it all into her new digs like a Chinese box. She was a cute old thing—she took a shine to me right off, giving me little winks on the sly—but it was clear things were getting a little fuzzy for her. I distinctly remember she kept calling Lamb "William" with an *I* for one thing, like she didn't remember or never knew it was the Dutch version, despite what he wrote about it. Also, she kept petting his hair like he was a cat or something—I mean, it was pink at the time, but still. Anyway, I settled in with the clicker to watch TV while he had his little visit. Luckily, she smoked too.

The crazy thing about that day actually came about six or so months later. Lamb's mom, Miranda, called me out of the blue. No *Hello how are you?*—she got right to the point, said she got my number from Lamb and had to ask me an important question.

"Did my mother give Lamb my father's gold watch?"

Apparently, Grandma forgot she had given the watch to him, couldn't remember later what happened to it at all, and so Miranda had accused Lamb of stealing it and didn't believe she'd given it to him—in fact, Grandma had insisted.

Miranda sounded pretty miffed even after I corroborated his story, which is probably why I still have the watch—it was in one of Lamb's boxes that I kept all these years, and I never felt the need to return it to her when I found it, wouldn't even know how to get in touch with her if I wanted to.

I found this little story about that day tucked away in one of his journals. About a year later, he mentioned to me that his Grandma died, so I think it was the last time he ever saw her, actually.

"The Watch on the Wall"

Willam Broeder

"Do you like it?" she asks, but she knows that I do, the watch on the wall, the gold watch engraved with a snail, a dragonfly, a beetle. It had stood on a table in her old house, hanging from a hook inside a bell jar, but since she's moved to the Hotel Chrysanthemum, a shelf on the wall near her chair is its new home. She can just turn her head, she says, to tell the time. She winds it every day.

We turn our heads now, look together. "It's a lot of fun—I've always thought so, since I was little."

This is true. The Art Nouveau watch has always fascinated me, heavy with gold, iridescent green and amber enamel. I only touched it once, three or four years old, when my grandmother lifted the glass and retrieved it to show my mother—a keepsake of a husband long dead, a grandfather before him, recently cleaned and repaired. I was allowed to hold it for barely a moment, my mother's hands hovering around mine, just long enough to feel its heft, then snatched back.

"It was your grandfather's, Willam," she says again, she always says. "It's yours now—I've never considered it mine, father to son—but I never had a son until you." (She means grandson.) The moment passes. My friend sits in the wing chair nearest the TV, glances at us furtively with the remote poised in his hand. The channel changes from flags and soldiers to tennis match. He sighs, sinks back, hiding.

"Pass me my cigarettes, my darling." ("Thank God!" cries the wing chair.)

I take a cigarette from my own pocket, too, but lean forward to light my grandmother's first. Her eyes flash her approval. She inhales gratefully. I light my own. (My friend revives, lights one too—ashtrays on every table.)

Eighty years distilled into two rooms and a kitchenette: furniture on furniture, shelf upon shelf; pictures and paintings, cheek by jowl; boxes and baubles; books and birdcages (empty, flown the coop.) And nestled within the center, powdered and rouged for her audience she sits, a babe again, wise and wizened. Ash dusts the table, dusts the chair arm, her sleeve. I imagine her slowly buried in ash, turned to ash herself, reach over to hold her hand.

"It's nice to see you," I say. "What are you reading?" I point at the yellowed paperback slipped between the cushion and the arm of her chair.

"Huxley!" she says with a wink. "It's your father's." (She means grandfather.) She glances at the watch. "Where can he be?" (He died in World War II.) "He doesn't like me to read his books, but I like to keep current." (Brave New World, 1932.)

Another, bigger sigh emerges from the wing chair. The channel changes again, cowboys under siege, arrows landing like lilies clasped to breasts.

"I wanted to tell you something," I say, "Mama doesn't want me to tell you, but..."

"That mouse—!" she laughs, shakes her head fondly. "To think I raised such a beige wit." She laughs even harder as I blink at her audacity. She nods toward the wing chair—Grande Dame Sees All. "He's very handsome—is it love?"

(A quizzical eye peeps round the edge of the chair.)

"Oh ... we're just friends."

"You could do worse," she says. ("Much worse!" agrees the echo.) "Tea?" ("Yes, please," says the echo.) She wants to rise but I stop her. I set the kettle on the doll stove, rummage through the cupboard. "Your father will have coffee." (She means grandfather, would have had.)

"Looks like we're out..."

"Of course. Curse this war. God damn this war!"

Three cups of tea, three more cigarettes. I rinse everything in the sink, set them to dry on the yellow towel. When I step back in the room, she's got the bell jar set aside, watch in hand.

"This is for you."

I shake my head. "No! No, I can't." She is insistent, almost angry at my refusal.

"But it's yours! He's always meant for you to have it—it was never mine, and it's certainly not your sister's." (She means mother.) "You must take it. He'll be upset if you don't. Please, honey." She puts it in my reluctant hand, closes my fingers around it. Her eyes are moist, soft again. She kisses us both on the cheek as we leave.

We're halfway down the hall when she calls after us. "Be careful out there, dears—don't let the butt flu get ya!" (She means AIDS.)

LAMB OF THE FLIES

You'd think that with Lamb going to private schools all his life, he would have had some clue about how to hold his own, but no—not a competitive bone in his body. In fairness, he had never attended a boarding school until Wolcott Academy. All through grade school in New York and the Netherlands, Switzerland for a while—wherever his father was posted—the schools had been day only, and co-ed, so he always had a gaggle of little girls fussing over him. But after his parents got divorced, his mom wanted him closer to her and her family in Los Angeles while she was between husbands (but not too close while she was hunting,) and Wolcott didn't go co-ed until a few years after we graduated.

Of course, I went to public school until sophomore year when it became obvious that if I wanted to go to college, the meager opportunities presented by the Antelope Valley School District weren't going to cut it. At least I was hardened by the reindeer games of a working class junior high and knew what was what. I had a keen eye for weaknesses and quick comebacks if anyone tried to pull anything, but Lamb? Totally defenseless, as evidenced by the nickname he acquired freshman year, and a key incident that happened early sophomore year around the time we started hanging out.

As nicknames go, Lamb really wasn't that bad compared to some others at Wolcott. A few of the older teachers still referred to students by their last names–Mr. Jaeger, Mr. Sykes, Mr. Fitzpatrick—so a lot of the guys were known that way (minus the *Mr.* of course,) with exceptions for brothers, and such obvious abbreviations as Fitz. But there was always room for embellishment.

A kid named Cunningham received the not unwelcome nickname of Lingus, thought it made him sound like a lady's man. One of the Batemans became Bator but couldn't protest too much because it was his own older brother who coined it, probably to keep it from being used on him. Brian Packer was completely unfazed by Pecker. An Andy who actually was caught playing with himself became Handy obviously, while a wretch with bad acne became Scarface. And then of course there was Bo Lam, the Chinese-American guy whose name turned into Lambo, to his utter delight, and finally Lamb, with the subtle twist on his actual name, Willam Broeder.

Anyway, with all these nicknames flying around and a bunch of new freshmen and sophomores, there was some confusion one day early on at lunch.

The dining hall was one of the original buildings from the school's founding in 1909, all creaky oak floors, wainscoting, big French windows looking out at the view of the coast, and a gigantic fireplace with the headmaster's table sitting pride of place in front.

This was the table where the seniors sat for regular lunches and dinners if the weather was crappy—the headmaster and other teachers only presided over these big round tables at formal dinners when everyone had to wear a jacket and tie. When the weather was good (which was usually) the seniors sat at picnic tables just outside on the senior lawn, and no one else was allowed to sit out there with them. Because of this tradition, we didn't usually sit specifically with our friends, but sorted by year with our classmates, so there might be three or four in a row occupied by juniors, another bunch by sophomores, and so on.

Remember, at fifteen, Lamb was six-three, and when he stood among us he seemed almost monstrous, in a class by himself. So this was the reason, I think, that Thomas, first name Jeffrey, a new sophomore like me, mistook Lamb for a junior as he was sitting down one of the first days of school. I was sitting at the other one, so I was a witness to all of this.

As Lamb set down his tray, Thomas—already playing alpha in our first week—said, "Wrong table, Lurch," which got a low rumble of laughter. "Go sit with the juniors."

But Lamb didn't hear who said it, and he told me later that he thought he said "Rich" not "Lurch" so he was thrown off. He said, "It's Lam—I'm a sophomore."

To which Thomas replied, "You're a sophomore? What the hell do they feed you?" This got an even bigger laugh, and Thomas ran with it. "What'd you say—what the fuck's your name?"

"Lamby!" someone yelled out.

"Lamby?" Thomas was beside himself with glee. "Get the fuck out."

So Lamb's first mistake was hesitating when he should have just sat down, and meanwhile, some new minion of Thomas's walked up behind him and was standing there now, expectant. All the boys were staring at him, waiting for his reaction, and Lamb said he got confused because he didn't recognize most of them—they were mostly all the new sophomores from a different dorm.

"Well, why don't you be polite and go start a new table, La-a-a-amb," said Thomas with a bleating noise. "This seat's saved for my friend here behind you." And then he actually shoved Lamb out of the way. "I said MOVE, jackass!" he hissed, and stepped in front of the empty chair so that Lamb would have had to shove him back to sit down.

At that moment, another boy got up from our table, and so, totally befuddled, Lamb picked up his tray and made way.

Big mistake.

That day, a heat whipped up at Thomas's table. Those first few weeks of a new year always began with a nervousness about them: a lot of boys were away from home for the first time. The freshmen were all new and unsure of themselves, and many of the new sophomores too didn't have the lay of the land yet.

And there absolutely were hierarchies at Wolcott Academy, as in life—seniors at the top, freshmen at the bottom, but a fair amount of wiggle room to stake out a claim in between. Which dorm you were in, whether you made junior varsity lacrosse (at least) and whether your voice had changed yet, whether you had pubic hair, or were still just a weenie. This last was of course exacerbated by the fact that the showers in the old dorms were still open, just one big room with many nozzles, and if you think that people weren't looking, you'd be wrong. (Guilty.)

That day at lunch developed swiftly into a resounding new world order centered around Thomas. The laughter and carousing rose and fell, and unlike most days with forgotten homework or quick games of foosball in the rec room beckoning, the boys surrounding him lingered as they realized they sat within the sphere of the emerging prince. Thomas, who had made varsity lacrosse the first day of tryouts. Thomas, who was from Emerald Bay, the gated community near Laguna. Thomas had a deep, bronze tan and sun-bleached hair from surfing all summer, and wore his madras shorts, neon tank top, and flip flops like some son of Apollo in human form. Thomas had a square jaw, a low, husky voice, and needed to shave every day since he arrived. Thomas was already a man at fifteen.

But as he drank in his new-found glory, Thomas continually darted glances over at Lamb, and I knew instantly he was figuring out how to squash one of the only boys who probably could beat him in a brawl if he'd had any backbone.

That was when I first noticed Lamb, saw his confusion and humiliation start to burn at him like acid as it dawned on him that he had just fought the first bout of a years-long match among these sons of soap opera actors, senators, chairmen of the boards of companies bearing their names—

and lost.

The hatred directed at Lamb would all finally come to a head two years later.

MR. PEREZ'S APARTMENT

Lamb kept diaries and journals from way before he went to Wolcott—there's a little green leather one with a lock on it written in Dutch, a child's scrawl. I haven't bothered with that one or some of the others because I have to hand type them into Google Translate, and a lot of the Dutch words are completely screwy. But later on, he used mostly English with some Dutch and French words thrown in now and then like he was trying to hide certain things in case someone read it.

The following entry was from sometime in the spring of our junior year. He wasn't too good about dates early on, and I don't remember exactly when it happened even though I remember that day. His handwriting was pretty terrible, and his punctuation even worse, but I got pretty good at reading his weird backward-slanting hieroglyphics from all his letters.

As far as the kissing stuff, well, I guess I can admit all

this time later that I could tell Lamb was falling in love with me. Even though I was seventeen and desperate to get my hands on some dick, I was afraid it would turn into some crazy situation where he couldn't turn it off, and then he'd let something slip and we'd get caught. I feel bad about it now, I mean, I think he got over it, but he never really could turn his feelings on and off.

He made one more try to kiss me later that year—I slugged him and told him to knock it off.

D wasn't really talking much that day—kinda strange because he's a talker—but he barely said two words as we were running around the track. Then right at the end when Mr. Hanna waved from up top of the ridge to let us know we were excused for the day, I said, "You wanna head into town?" It was half-day Saturday, so we had all afternoon to hang out. I was jonesing for a ciggy.

"Yeah, but I want to do something first." D started walking toward the Bachelor Barn, so I followed.

"What are we doing?"

"I just want to see something," he said, and I thought Oh, he wants to ask Mr. Perez something about Spanish homework but then I remembered the soccer team had an away game and he wouldn't be back until late. So we walked around to the front and he started turning door knobs. There are three apartments, but Mr. Perez is the only teacher living in the Barn this year, so D tried two of the doors and they were locked, but the third one was unlocked.

"Here we go," he said, and he walked straight in!

"D, what the fuck?"

"Shut up!" he said, and grabbed me and pulled me in with him and closed the door. It isn't huge, just a living room and little kitchen, a bathroom, and in the back corner, a bedroom area with a pony wall separating it.

Mr. Perez is kinda messy—the bed wasn't made. Funny because we have to make our beds every morning. There were dishes piled up in the sink, looked like mostly cereal bowls, and some empty pizza boxes stacked next to the trash can. His surfboard was on the table, and there was a puck of Mr. Zog's Sex Wax sitting on top. His wetsuit was slung over one of the chairs.

D hardly looked around at all, he left me by the door and went straight through to the dresser by the bed and started opening drawers.

I said, "Seriously, what the fuck?" and he stopped and glared at me like I was getting on his nerves (I'm used to it.)

"Perez is a stoner, I fucking know it—he talks about the Grateful Dead all the time in class, and he's been trading bootleg tapes of Dead shows with Thomas and his posse— look!" He pointed to the shelf with Mr. Perez's stereo, and sure enough, he's got a whole rack of cassettes with handprinted dates, decorated with little skulls and lightning bolts and stuff. "If he drops acid, he smokes weed, and I want some, that's what the fuck!"

He's always like this, dragging me into things without really asking—it's why we got caught smoking on my balcony after lights out and had to spend three Saturdays doing detention clearing brush out by the old pump house. I guess it's not D's fault I started smoking, but I only used to sneak cigarettes now and then. Seems like he was already smoking with his brother by the time he got to Wolcott, and then pretty soon we're lighting up every chance we get, and by the time I went home to my mom's last summer, I couldn't stop.

So D was poking through Mr. Perez's drawers, and then he said, "A-ha," and pulled out two cartons of Camel Reds—one of them was open. I told him not to but he started unwrapping a pack.

"He'll never know." But then he stopped. "Whoa, look at this—"

He waved me over—I was still by the door, super nervous—but I went and there were a bunch of nudie mags, only not just Playboy and Hustler, but other ones with guys on the cover, Honcho and Bunk House Boys and shit like that. D's like "Holy fuck! Jackpot!" and he sits down on the bed and starts looking through them.

I told him to hurry up, and he shushed me. "What if someone comes?" He rolled his eyes and walked over to the kitchen—there were about five open bottles of tequila on the counter, different brands, and he unscrewed one of them and took a swig. He told me to sit down, and handed me the bottle, so I took a sip. Then he rummaged through the bedside table and pulled out a big bag of weed. There was a plate with a bunch of shake and some rolling papers, and he handed it to me, and said, "Roll us a joint," but I don't really know how and my hands were shaking I was so worried about getting caught.

D kept pulling on the tequila bottle and then he walked over and put the one we'd been drinking from back and grabbed another one. "We can't drink too much from just one."

I still hadn't rolled a joint. "You're useless." He grabbed the plate from me and put it back in the drawer, and he took some from the bag and rolled it up in a paper towel and stuck it in his pocket. Then he came back to sit on the bed next to me and started looking at the magazines again. I laid back on the bed—the tequila made me feel a little sick but also warm. I felt something next to my hand tangled up in the sheets, and when I pulled it out, it was a jockstrap.

"Jesus! Perez's jockstrap—give me that." D took it and sniffed it. I said "Gross! Stop—" but next thing I know D's got his hand down my pants, and he's pulling down my shorts and started sucking me off!

I didn't know what to do. A couple of times when we were hanging out after lights out, I was stretched out on my bed and D laid down next to me and said he was just going to shut his eyes for a minute but don't let him fall asleep. He laid down so my hand was underneath his crotch, and I was too afraid to move but I could feel him getting hard and I froze.

This time was different, like he was full on going for it, but I was super scared and my hands were shaking. I didn't move, and I wasn't getting hard so he was sucking on my worm and after a minute he stopped and said, "Ugh, what the hell is wrong with you? Go outside and keep watch. You're bumming me out."

I felt ashamed. I pulled up my shorts and stood outside like he told me.

Why won't he kiss me? Isn't that how it's supposed to go? I tried to kiss him that first time in bed but he turned his head away.

After a few minutes the tequila was really starting to hit me, and I tried to work up the nerve to go back in and see if we could try again but all of a sudden Thomas walked around the corner!

He almost stopped in his tracks, but then kept coming. I was so nervous I almost heaved. I called out "Hey Thomas!" loud so D wouldn't walk out, and Thomas said, "What the fuck are you doing here?" All I could think to say was that I wanted to ask Mr. Perez a Spanish question, and Thomas looked at me funny. "He's got an away game."

I said, "Oh right, I forgot" and then added, "Why aren't you with them?" because Thomas is on the varsity soccer team.

"My sister's getting married, my parents are coming to pick me up."

And then I asked, "Do you know the Spanish homework for Monday?"

"I'm in Spanish 2,"—I'm in Spanish 3—and he said, "I was going to ask him the same thing."

"He's not here," I said.

"No shit," he said, "I just told you." He walked off giving me the side eye. I peeked around the corner of the Barn and made sure he was really leaving, and then I went back and knocked on Perez's door just to be sure D was done with whatever he was doing, and he opened the door right away.

"Fuck that was close," he said, and we walked back to the dorm to shower and change, and caught the next shuttle down to town.

We usually smoke behind 7-Eleven after we buy a

pack, but since we already had the one he stole from Perez, we went straight down to the beach and bought Cokes from the hotdog stand. He finished his quick, and then he pulled a tack out of his pocket, squeezed the can so there was a groove and poked a bunch of holes in the side of it— can bong—I've never seen that before. You put a little bud on top over the holes and then suck through the opening. I got one hit and then my hand jerked and the bud fell off still smoldering on the ground. D yelled at me and picked it up and wouldn't let me hold it after that, just held it and lit it for me.

We had a great afternoon smoking and eating hotdogs and more Cokes, we laughed our asses off, but we didn't talk about what happened at Perez's apartment, except for why Thomas came down to the Barn if he already knew Perez was at an away game.

THE FIRE ROAD PART I

Of all the stories I found in Lamb's papers, the one he titled "The Fire Road" was by far the longest, and the most disturbing. He used some of the events of our time at Wolcott, but most of it is a total fantasy. There was in fact a kid who called the school pretending to be his dad so he could pull out of a school-sponsored field trip and go surfing in Baja for the summer.

What's weird is that Lamb used people's real names, and the name of our school, which I've changed to keep some semblance of anonymity. Anyone who went to school with us could probably recognize it, and even some of their classmates in the characters. But I also wouldn't be surprised if none of them remember a damn thing about what they put Lamb through. Anyway, where Lamb used real names, I've changed them to the names I've been using—like Thomas, and "Wolcott Academy" itself.

This story reminds me of those kids who shot up

Columbine. I dated a guy who went to Columbine a couple years after, and he said that despite all these experts and investigators saying 'No, no, bullying didn't cause them to snap' it was common knowledge that both those kids were called 'faggot' and 'queer' for years, and at one point they had shit flung at them. We bury our heads in the sand about what complete dicks guys can be, then offer up thoughts and prayers when some poor kid loses it.

Still, I prefer the idea of writing a revenge story than going on a murder spree. Oh, Lamb—sometimes I feel like I didn't know you at all.

"The Fire Road"

Willam Broeder

Paralysis grips you where you stand. The knobs of the dresser press into your legs. They are someone else's legs feeling the sharp points. Burke, Andrews and Moore slouch snickering on your bed and trunk. Thomas sits at your desk. He rifles through your drawers and papers as though looking for something. Your dorm room stinks of their lacrosse practice sweat. Their rapaciousness. It is two hours yet until dinner, and Penny won't be opening the snack bar for another thirty minutes. They are hungry.

"So?" Thomas says. He fixes you with a smirk, half ingratiating and half something else. "You going to make me search for it? Don't be stingy, Markenstein—I know you've got food."

You haven't been this close to Thomas since last year. He's grown, filled out. You can't help but notice the tan lines as his boxers ride up his lean thighs. His robe falls open. He was on his way to the shower. He has a dusting of fuzz on his chest and stomach.

Burke pulls his muddy cleats up onto your bedcover. He echoes the taunt. "Yeah, dude, don't be stingy—everyone knows you brought a care package back from mommy."

You did bring a box from home yesterday, yes, some food. Mostly just things you wanted for your dorm room. Just a few. The narrow cell is less than half the size of your room at home. Your mom slipped a box of Pop-Tarts in with your posters and shoes, and a new radio alarm clock to replace the crystal one she rescued from the attic and sent with you the first week. One word from the strange boy next door—Matt—and you knew you needed something less conspicuous.

The Pop-Tarts, then. You pull open your closet door and retrieve the unopened box.

"Now we're talking," Thomas says. He rips it from your hand and passes out the foil packages. "What else you hiding in there?"

You can't remember, now. The tense knot of fear grips you. You turn back to peer inside your closet, sight and thought disconnected.

"Chips!" cries Andrews.

"And cookies! Fucker!" Moore hisses. They shove you aside and help themselves, tearing into the packages like only dogs and teenage boys can.

You study the knotted pine paneling. The mud on your coverlet. You cough. A bell rings in your ears. The last Pop-Tart lands on the floor, carelessly trampled under a cleated foot. You press yourself against the dresser again, seek out the knobs, the points of them against your back. You are somewhere, anywhere, else.

There is a knock at the door. As it swings open you are trapped behind it against the dresser, too frozen to move.

"Where's Mark?" a voice asks.

"He's not here," says Thomas. He is staring right at you as he says it, a cold mirth in his eye.

The voice persists. "Then what the fuck are you doing in here?"

You stir from behind the door and peek around. It's your neighbor, Matt. "I'm here," you croak.

One by one the others stand and file sheepishly out. All but Thomas. He upends the bag of chips, empties the last crumbs into his mouth. "Thanks, dude—hey, you can get more, right? Your mom makes a great chocolate cake I seem to remember."

You can't stop yourself. "I can ask."

Thomas swaggers out the door toward the showers. "Yeah, do that," he says over his shoulder. "And get some air freshener for your room or something, dude, it fucking stinks like cat piss in there."

Matt surveys the mess of empty packages and crumbs as you stand dumbly by. He shakes his head, frowning. "You can't let them do that to you."

"It's alright, I can always get more," you say.

Matt sniffs. He smells it too. Not the sweat and the dirty socks and the mud—the fear. You reek of it. He looks away from the glassy stare of your eyes. You are hard to look at. He says he heard the clamor as he passed by, wondered what was up. You are usually quiet.

You've made no friends in the dorm yet. You made none the year before when you were only a freshman day student. You would come to classes in the morning, but go home for lunch. At the end of each day you booked it back down the winding asphalt curve to your house. Boarding is supposed to get you out of your shell this year.

Matt is a new sophomore. He's seen you walking back and forth under the eucalyptus trees to the big old ranch house just visible at the end of the road, across the soccer field. Someone told him your mom is the granddaughter of the founder of the school, and still a trustee, is that true? Your dad runs the family's avocado ranch.

Matt tells you to snap out of it, wake up, get a grip. The trick is not to think about it. If someone gives you shit, you just sling it right back. Find the chink in the armor and skewer the bastard.

"I don't want to hurt anyone," you say.

He scoffs. "Dude could stand to get hurt." He'd like to see that, says Thomas may be quick, and no push over, but you've got nearly a foot and fifty pounds on him. "You're not afraid to hurt, you're afraid to get hurt."

Thomas, though. "That guy is too good-looking for his own good." You're surprised that he says it. Thomas is a bully and sneering prick. Your neighbor wonders what he'd look like stripped down and tied to a tree, gagged and afraid. His defiance thrills you.

It was a mistake to promise them more. You berate yourself, and your steps turn to stomps on the thin ribbon of road back home. But your pounding heart slows. The breeze across your flushed face is cold. Feels good. Your shoe slips on the gumnuts under the eucalyptus trees, but you are still hopped up on adrenaline and barely feel your knee contact the asphalt. Up and on you walk, barely a pause.

What will you say? A gang of boys ate all your food. You must offer them more. Maybe they'll like you, or at least not hate you. You are ridiculous.

The rake of the last rays of the setting sun cast immense shadows. You are stretched into the distance, flitting between the dusk-red blanks of the trees, one moment infinite, the next truncated. Big, little, big, little. You can't stay long. Everyone will be heading to dinner. It is only a ten-minute walk, home and back. The porch light flicks on. You squeeze between the Volvo and the oleander along the drive. If you're lucky, they'll all be watching TV. Sneak in, sneak out, none the wiser. You are not lucky tonight.

"Sweetheart! Oh good, you're just in time for dinner." Your mom kisses you. She waves her hand toward the family room. "Your dad's watching golf, Brett is upstairs. I'll just add another setting to the table." She turns and bustles. No getting out of it without a battle.

Pots simmer on the big, old range. You flick on the stove light. Chicken and brussel sprouts roasting. Potatoes boiling. Bacon sizzles with walnuts and butter. Better than the broccoli spears rolled in sliced turkey on the dining hall menu. You steal a sliver of bacon. You catch a glimpse of your father through the doorway.

Adam Stern has a hearing problem. He refuses to admit it. Each year he turns up the volume of TVs, radios, and his own voice. It's a regular din. It's a Stern family thing. You wonder if you too will go deaf, be one of those loud, shouting Sterns. You will sit in company and feign interest without hearing a word that is said. Your dad has learned to read lips, to give his full attention when someone is speaking to him to discern what they say, or look away if he's annoyed. You insert yourself between TV and easy chair to capture his attention.

"Mark! Son!" Everything a yell. "You staying for dinner?" You nod *yes*. He grapples with the remote control to mute the roar of announcers and spectators at a tournament in Hawaii. You vacationed once on Maui just so he could play on the famed Kapalua course. "How's dorm life?"

Your father was eager for you to live in the dorms

freshman year. Your mother said *no*. You weren't ready. She still remembers a time when there was no hot water in the showers, and Bible study was mandatory—days long past. She felt sorry for the miserable boys in school jackets and ties. "I remember too—I was one of them," he'd said, an old Wolcott boy himself.

"It's OK," you say. You glance at your dad, and away, try not to betray the tightrope of feelings.

"Well, you look great, son, I think you've grown just in the last month. Where's a pencil? Elanor! We need a pencil!" You shake your head. Wave both hands *No!* Has it been a year since he marked your height on the doorjamb?

Your mother pops her head around the corner. "Maybe after dinner, hon."

"You've got to be the tallest fifteen I ever saw," he goes on. He clears the paper from the sofa beside him. You sit in the chair.

"Remember me what classes you're taking? You're not in algebra with old Sandy Miller?"

Pre-calculus.

"No! Already? I don't think we even had precalculus back in my day." You'll do fine, just fine, he's sure. "How's your tennis swing coming along...?" You aren't playing tennis.

He's off and running about his glory days at Wolcott, shining on the hill. All roads led back to the headmaster's pretty daughter. He did a stint teaching American history after college to be near her. "Who would I even be?" he asks. "Elanor Wolcott Stern made me the man I am today. Out of a handful of dust from Bakersfield. Into an avocado farmer!" He sounds surprised.

This stiff but affable man. He embarrasses you. "Get a hearing aid, Dad!" your brother Brett always yells at him. He won't hear of it. Up at sunrise every morning with the workers—checking trees and irrigation, spraying, pruning, harvesting, packaging, testing. He loves his trees almost as much as he loves his sons. Trees don't talk.

"...And I said 'Goddamn it, if that pipe's not fixed by Friday, the whole back forty will dry up and waste the crop, so you better—'"

"Dinner!" Elanor screams from the kitchen. He starts, struggles upright, shambles off toward the dining room with his paper in tow. It's his habit. Buried in the sports page to the relief of everyone or he'd be interrupting every other word with "What? What?" as you try to tell each other about your days.

You move to follow him, but your mom asks you to drag Brett out of his room. She doesn't care if he skips it when it's just the three of them, "...but he'd damn well better get his butt to the table when his brother is home from school!"

Where you are gangly, withdrawn, wincing, your younger brother is powerful, self-assured, forthright. As though the first try went awry, the next more sure of its mark. He smiles broadly when you knock on the open door. He takes off his headphones and pulls a chair beside his own. He is playing Super Mario Bros. on his Nintendo.

"I already messed up this game—I can start again with two-player. I'll let you be Mario."

You sit. You don't take the other joystick. You pick up a Rubik's Cube and spin it. With each step to put yourself in order, you are further from the solution. Brett starts his game over, slouches deeper into his chair.

"What's up, big brother? You're off—I can feel it."

Two years separate you. Brett will start Wolcott next year. He'll be the captain of every team. You can barely believe you are brothers.

You admit to Brett the episode in your room. You never take your eyes off the spinning cube. You can solve one side, but never get a second.

"You've got yourself a bully." Brett says it matter-of-factly, like it's a simple thing. He tosses aside his joystick and snatches the cube away. "Who's on your team?" He spins the sides of the cube.

"Team?"

"Well it's four against one, sounds like—how are you supposed to even compete, much less win, if you're playing by yourself?"

You've never understood it that way. Leave it to your little brother to come up with the obvious solution you couldn't see.

"I'm not sure there's anyone on my team."

Brett whistles, bent over the cube, spinning furiously. "There's your problem right there. It's a game, Mark. There are rules. First rule: Find allies."

This is a revelation. "But no one even really talks to me."

"Well don't wait for someone to talk to you. Talk to them."

"I don't know what to say."

Brett sighs loudly. Larger blocks of solid color slowly emerge on the cube in his hands. "Don't say anything, then—ask questions. You don't even need to say something specific, you can use the same questions on everyone.

'Where are you from?' 'Do you have any pets?' 'Did you do the homework yet?' It's not rocket science, Mark. 'What movies did you see over the summer?' Easy."

You could give it a try.

"Mom shouldn't have let you stay home last year—it was too easy for you to hunker down and scurry home after classes. Plus you don't have sports—that's the easiest way to make friends, usually."

His hands are a blur. "Isn't there anyone? You don't have to marry him, dingdong, you just have to not be alone when these dicks come knocking. That's always the first order of business: say 'Hi' to someone. Be part of a herd. Bullies always pick off the stragglers. It's true of lions, it's true of people."

You nod your head slowly, light beginning to dawn. "There is one guy. Matt. He seems to want to help."

"Ha! Two steps ahead of me, big brother. Well, go track him down when you get back and ask him for help on your homework or whatever."

"I don't need help."

"And one step back..." Brett rolls his eyes. "Why are you here, anyway?"

"It's time for dinner."

With a final twist, Brett sets the completed cube down in front of you.

"Oh, but sweetheart, it's no problem at all—I made two." She insists. "I was going to freeze one—you can never have too many emergency cakes—but I'll just wrap it in some foil and you can take it back with you to share with your friends. It's not iced, but it's fine just plain."

"Mom, no. Please..." you say again, up to your elbows in dish suds. She ignores you, fishes in the drawer for the box of foil.

Brett snickers as he dries a pot. "She's setting you up." But Elanor refuses to listen, slices off one aluminum sheet, finds it too short, pulls off another, this one too long. Wraps the cake up like a metal mummy.

"Your friend Jason really liked my chocolate cake when he and his parents came for dinner. He'll be happy," she says. She means Thomas. Jason is his first name.

It is after all what you came home to get, a peace offering that now feels like protection money. Brett grabs a pot from your hands while it's still dripping and leans in. "You could offer some to Matt," he whispers, "but be cool, you know. Off handed."

OK.

"Cool. Be cool," Brett reiterates.

"OK!" You finish the last pot, wipe your hands, receive the bag with cake. "Do we have any more Pop-Tarts?"

Elanor is *that* kind of mom—a big pantry filled to the rafters with every kind of everything, cans and boxes and packages. "What kind?"

"Maybe strawberry, or brown sugar cinnamon?" She hunts down your selections.

"I thought you don't like the strawberry ones."

You shrug. "I don't."

She shifts a shelf full of cereal to access a hidden stash. "Your father would live on these if I didn't hide them." She drops two boxes in your bag, and adds an unopened package of Oreos.

"Thanks, Mom." You kiss her cheek. Nod at Brett. "Bye,

Dad!" you scream at the family room.

"What?!" he yells back.

"See you later!"

"OK, sounds good!"

"Mark, sweetheart, can you just help me in the shed real quick before you go?"

You follow her out the French doors, down the brick path. Together you throw open the windows so the garden shed airs out.

It's actually the big old ranch kitchen, converted. No party at Elanor and Adam's is complete without a ladies' walk-through. Through the rose garden to the old kitchen where her grandmother cooked pueblo-style in an open porch for everyone, back when the workers grew mainly citrus and the alligator pear was still a novelty. "You call this a shed, Elanor?" some trustee or faculty wife always cries out incredulously. You, dutiful son, always make the rounds with her and the guests.

She lays a hand on your shoulder. She points from the big farmhouse worktable to the top shelf above the crystal and ceramic vases she collects. "Help me with these jugs?"

When they first were married and Adam took over management of the ranch, she insisted he rip out half an acre of the avocados so she could have a proper orchard, as much for the branches as the fruit. "Oh! What fruit!" people always say in the spring. But she will confess, "I couldn't care less if they bear fruit or not." Huge sprays and oversized bouquets of flowering branches are her signature decorating move. Her own mother grew up on an apple farm. She learned from her how to cut and force fruit branches to blossom in these heavy stoneware jugs.

You convey the earthenware as she wipes down the table and counters. She stops for a moment to look at you intently. You can't look her in the eye.

"How are you really doing, sweetheart? You're more quiet than usual, if that's even possible."

You continue sorting and rearranging not only the top but the lower shelves. It's your job to keep the shed looking just so. Clean the tools after she spends time in the garden. Buff each windowpane with a newspaper after washing to make sure they sparkle. It was you who lightly distressed the new tile floor with a bike chain. You smeared and buffed it with brown shoe polish until it looked medieval— your summer project last year.

"Sweetheart. Say something."

"Not sure what you want me to say."

"How about 'I'm great' or 'I'm miserable' or whatever you like, but talk to me. A mother can tell—"

"I'm great," you say abruptly, "and I should get going. Study hall starts in half an hour."

She stalls. "Can you take down those bundles there?" She grows all her own herbs. Lavender. Sage. Rosemary. She hangs them to dry from the low beams she salvaged from the old horse barn on campus, finally dismantled long after the riding program was discontinued. A curious student got tetanus from a rusty nail in the crumbling hulk.

You sigh.

She will draw this out, hoping to draw you out. "Can you put that bucket up here on the table?" The trestle work-table is also built from planks out of the old horse barn. You lift the bucket full of Japanese maple branches. The crimson red leaves will look great in the front hall.

"You're going to make me late," you say. She waves the suggestion away.

"I still pull a little weight around here, you know, I can send you back with a note."

You sigh. "I wish you wouldn't."

"You don't have to go back at all, if you don't want." She fiddles with the bucket and the branches. Not looking at you might make the suggestion more palatable.

"What, move back home after a month?"

She shrugs. "Why not? If you're not happy…"

And a part of you is thrilled to hear her say it. You are tempted.

"I think I need to stick it out." You're armed with Brett's advice. You will say something to Matt. You will share your mother's cake with the funny kid who also seems friendless but completely unfazed and untouched by the others. Matt plays lacrosse, quite well by all accounts. "I can always switch back to day next year if it doesn't work out."

She offers a smile. "Alright. It's up to you, sweetheart. You know I'm just three steps away—and Brett, and Daddy too."

You are late for study hours. The house teacher is aware of your special circumstances. Elanor isn't the only Wolcott sitting on the Board of Trustees, but she is the only one living on campus, and the acknowledged Mother of Wolcott Academy. They turn to her for every occasion.

You pop your head into Matt's room to invite him for cake. You hope you sound breezy. But the stony silence of your neighbor is unnerving. You retreat. It might be a challenge to enlist him as an ally if you have nothing to say to one another. You wonder if this strategy will work.

You sit at your desk. Organize the papers and books Thomas scattered around. You are too anxious to study. Mostly it is reading homework. Martin Luther's Reformation. Shakespeare's *Twelfth Night* for English. You can catch up over the weekend. Studying is easier at home. You have a special dispensation to stay at home Saturday nights whenever you want.

When study hours end, you are just beginning to dig into Act Two. You are surprised it is half past nine already. You wander next door to Matt's room. He's not there. Maybe the blank look on his face meant he was lost in thought. Maybe he didn't understand you have cake. You go to Penny's to find him.

You never spend much time in the rec room. There's a TV but it's never turned to any show you like. You have no one in particular to play pool, ping pong, or foosball with. Home is so close. You don't depend on Penny's snacks like many of the boys do. Some get care packages, or shop down at the grocery store in town. Those who forget to plan ahead are caught short, eager for her bagel dogs and burritos, even if they are microwaved. It isn't a place you like to hang out. You wouldn't be here now if it weren't for Brett's encouragement. You pull open the door to the basement lair. It exhales pizza rolls in your face.

You are barely in the door when you notice Thomas and friends milling around the pool table. You station yourself behind a pillar by the tables where kids play chess and Risk. Where is Matt? You don't see him. You pretend to watch a chess game just starting. If there is any group on campus you are likely to join, it would have been Chess Club. But they impressed on you at the first meeting that it is for serious students of strategy and openings. You know nothing about those.

You stay behind the column, hiding behind a couple guys who are also observing. You see Matt on a stool by the vending machines watching the pool game from a distance. You will have to make yourself visible to go talk to him. You are safe enough in a crowd. You go up to the vending machine. As you pretend to make a selection, the moaning begins.

"Markensteiiiiiin..."

Just one voice, and then another, repeats it again.

"Markensteiiiiiin..." Low and guttural, they growl out this new nickname Thomas invented, louder and louder with each refrain. Blood rushes to your head. Your heartbeat pounds in your face and ears as they taunt.

"Markensteiiiiiin..." Howling now, they put their arms out stiff, in that monster way. They mill around each other. "Markensteiiiiiin..." Others notice the fun. They laugh and join in. The whole room fills with this zombie noise. Penny shrieks out, "Shut up, you boys!"

You are humiliated. You turn tail and walk straight back out of the rec room.

What a cheap shot, Matt says, ganging up on you like that. The way they groaned out that nasty nickname, some kind of joke about how tall you are. Dick move.

He'd known Wolcott had a reputation for being the favorite school of rich assholes. He wouldn't have chosen it except for the trouble freshman year. Down in L.A.

Buckley didn't invite him back. He might have spent a free period pounding nails in the tires of every other Mercedes one afternoon. Maybe he'd been caught smoking a joint. Maybe he wanted to get kicked out of Terry's alma mater. If he'd had to hear one more senior girl drawl, "I knew your brother before ... You know..." he might have had to burn down the school.

They were talking about you at dinner. He sat at the next table from Thomas and his posse. Whenever possible, he sits at a different sophomore table from that prick. Yes, he hates a bully, but it's something else. He caught Thomas glaring at him once in history. He'd contradicted something Thomas said.

"History didn't start with Jesus, dude," Matt replied. The whole idea of "biblical scholars" was moronic. It's all a complete fiction. Thomas had been flustered. He backtracked on his own statement that the Roman Catholic Church was the foundation of Western thought. What a joke.

The way Thomas is treating you is obviously a cover for his own insecurity. The fact that you had hung out a couple of times made you a surrogate target, a way for Thomas to strike back without confronting him personally. Putz.

Problem is most of the guys think Thomas is the greatest thing since sliced bread. Burke and Moore were yucking it up on either side of him at dinner. They ate up every word he said.

There's something wrong with you, Thomas was saying. He tossed a roasted potato at the freshman table next to theirs. "I don't care if his great-grandfather was the original Wolcott. His dad's deaf, maybe that's it—maybe that's

Markenstein's problem. He's a little deaf, too." This was received with great amusement. Then Thomas mouthed "Markenstein" with that nasal enunciation like a deaf person might make. Everyone lost it. They kept it up through dinner, and all the way back to the dorm for study hours.

Matt was furious. He couldn't concentrate back in his own room. It boiled his blood. That jackass getting so much attention. He was too irritated to study. He hid his copy of *One Flew Over the Cuckoo's Nest* inside his history book in case the teacher on duty walked in. He'd found it in his brother's room, after ... Well, never mind. He'd already used up two of his three weekends at home for the semester because his mom got lonely in the house down in town—since the divorce, since everything that happened.

Then you knocked and poked your head in. Something about cake. He didn't reply, half in thought, and you retreated before he had a chance to say anything. You're like a beaten dog, shying away from a raised hand.

The minute study hours ended, he raced to Penny's to be first in line for a burrito and a Coke. The Turkey Surprise for dinner made him want to puke. Penny is the groundskeeper's wife? She takes a lot of shit from these spoiled brats. They mock the way she calls out "Burrito!" and generally act like assholes because she drives an ancient station wagon and works for a living. Thomas is always the first to pipe up with a shrill echo whenever she calls out someone's order.

Fuck, he hates him. What a complete dick. It doesn't matter that he's good-looking. Doesn't matter that he's on the varsity lacrosse team already. Even worse, Mr. Stalling thinks he's the golden child. If there's one thing he hates, it's how Stalling fawns over Thomas and crew during class, laughing at his jokes, bonding on the field. He wonders if Stalling is queer. Maybe he has a crush on Thomas, secretly wants to get in good with the kid. Who knows what might happen on an overnight trip to an away game. It makes him sick to think of it. Stalling is in his fifties, and acts like a giddy kid as soon as Thomas walks into class. Disgusting.

He was eating a burrito, wedged into a corner by the vending machines. He was watching Thomas and minions when you walked in. He saw the whole thing. He is going to make sure Thomas regrets what he did to you.

Matt's a real talker once he gets going.

CRUSHING

I've got to hand it to Lamb: the one time he went after a guy, he went gung ho. His courage must have been a beginner's faith because it was not long after we made a pact to come out for real. Up until that point, we were only out to each other, but it was actually Lamb who suggested we make it official after we both moved out of the dorms for fall semester junior year, him at Cal and me at USC.

Lamb's friend Lindsey introduced him to this little 18+ gay club called The Mix on Shattuck Avenue in Berkeley. She had met a lesbian chick named Darla in one of her classes—they started hanging out and then invited Lamb to go out one Saturday night. Anyway, Fugie was friends with Darla, and between them they knew everyone. That was the same summer I came up to visit when Fugie gave me his cockamamie story about being recruited by the psychic institute when he was a kid.

Lamb had started dying his hair crazy colors, and had a

real, proper mohawk. Six-feet-six, and another nine inches to the tips of his spikes, he was too much for any of those baby queers to handle, and since he was still his shy, aloof self—his sort of morbid limbo after his breakdown our senior year at Wolcott—there was a lot of *look but don't touch* going on when he first arrived on the arm of a straight girl. Everyone was friendly, but no one knew what to do with him.

"His name is Arthur." That was the message Lamb left me one day on my answering machine. Nothing else, but I knew him and his little crushes well enough to guess that he was smitten, and I called him back that evening for the scoop.

It was one of those beauty from afar situations. Lamb had seen this guy at The Mix a couple times that summer, and it turned out they had a class together in the fall—Econ 1, one of those big breadth courses that Lamb kept missing because there was always a waiting list jammed with business and econ majors who needed to get it out of the way before they took any other classes. Apparently, it took a month or two for Lamb to spot Arthur among the 800 other students in Zellerbach Auditorium, not only because of the size of the class, but also because Arthur had a bit of a Jekyll and Hyde persona, on and off campus.

Arthur was without a doubt one of the prettiest boys I ever laid eyes on, even when he was just slouching around Telegraph and hanging upstairs at café Milano with Lamb and friends. He had this incredibly smoldering look about him, with perfect Latin skin and thick dark hair he wore long and messy, like one of the Lost Boys from the movie— we probably watched that a hundred times. In the bright light of day, Arthur was not super flamboyant—he was smart, and he seemed serious about getting good grades and stuff.

But out at the clubs? I had never met a guy who wore full-on makeup, like mascara, eyeliner, eyeshadow, lipstick—other than drag queens of course—but when Arthur wore makeup he was devastating, like Jack Sparrow but with good teeth and better dressed. Not a full face like foundation and all that, and maybe it was more of a tinted lip gloss than lipstick? I don't know, that's never been my thing, but Jesus, you never saw such a sultry spectacle when he was *On*.

I think that's what caught Lamb's attention from the get-go: while every other queen was trying to butch it up and blend in with the other clones, Arthur was G.L.A.M.— Dionysos incarnate. I totally get why Lamb fell for him, hard.

It was a slow burn at first because Arthur had an on again/off again boyfriend—they were *off* when Lamb was first introduced, and he was completely mesmerized until he finally laid eyes on Craig, the little gym bunny boy-friend. Lamb couldn't be more different. Was Craig even five feet tall? He was a pocket gay, for sure—Arthur himself was about six feet, and Lamb fretted that if he liked throwing a tight half-pint around, then his own doughy six-six was probably not on the menu.

As Lamb started hanging around with that gang, he kept hoping every time Arthur and Craig had a fight that maybe he could turn Arthur's head. He didn't go crazy exactly, but there was a steady beat of little gifts and cards for birthdays and Christmas. I'd say they actually seemed to be best friends on the surface, to the point that I got tired of hearing about Arthur, but I knew that Lamb had an obsession simmering.

On Valentine's Day, Arthur damned Craig to hell once and for all. He seemed to be finally warming up to Lamb, but when he asked if hooking up meant they would be exclusive and Lamb said he had no interest in anyone else, Arthur bugged out back to Craig and disappeared during the spring break Lamb had invited him to drive down to SoCal for a party week with me. Needless to say, spring break was spring broke.

The following summer was a big one because me and Lamb were both finally 21 and could get into the real clubs in the City—suddenly, The Mix was for kids. I spent a lot of weekends up in Berkeley, and we were going into the City Saturday nights to Colossus, then the End Up afterwards, back to Lamb's to sleep during the day like vampires, and if I didn't have to be back in L.A. early Monday, we'd be at Pleasuredome Sunday night too.

We still saw Arthur out and about most weekends, but Lamb was licking his wounds and I pushed him into the arms of whatever dude seemed halfway interested to try and get him over it. Unfortunately, this backfired, and turned into a series of one-sided crushes over the next year or two. Lamb would go home with a guy, and then obsess over him for the next however many months until he got ghosted.

"What happened this time?" I'd ask. "What did he say?"

Mark: "He said I'm too serious."

Carlos: "He said he's not ready to tie himself down."

Jerry: "Sex wasn't hot enough."

Jeff: "Do I smell weird?"

Grady: "Nothing, he just stopped returning my calls."

Not too long after Lamb went to bartending school and got his first job at The Club, this hole-in-the-wall bar South of Market, who shows up but Arthur. They were both a couple years out of school by then, and although Arthur was working the door at Product, or maybe it was Trannyshack, I don't think he had a real job so I suspect he was dealing drugs and pretty much partying all the time.

Lamb still had no boyfriend, and so when Arthur started hanging around weeknights at the bar and acting all friendly and trying to reconnect, of course Lamb ate it up. I would stop in for an hour or two once in a while just to keep him company because it could be pretty slow, and Arthur would chat us up and slowly get more and more wasted.

What I noticed were the little strokes on Lamb's hand (instead of tips) as he handed Arthur his drinks. Eventually, he started showing up without any cash (*Oh shit! I lost/forgot my wallet!*) and asking to borrow from Lamb, who meanwhile was talking again like he had a chance in hell and no idea that Arthur was just using him for free booze.

One night, the owner of the bar was filling in for another bartender, and was standing right next to Lamb when Arthur tried to take his Jack and Coke without paying for it. The guy yelled at him, "Dude, what the fuck are you doing?" and Arthur turns back and glares at Lamb like he had betrayed him. I guess he only had a buck or two in his wallet and just threw it on the bar and dashed away with the drink, so the owner tossed him out and told him he was barred.

A week later, Lamb got a box in the mail. Inside were all the cards and trinkets Lamb had ever given Arthur since they'd been friends, all torn up. A T-shirt Lamb had given him was cut to shreds. He also started getting all these magazines, like a subscription bomb with all these invoices due, and we knew it was Arthur because the address labels all had the same wrong zip code he used on the "gift" box.

About a month after that, Lamb got woken up by someone ringing his bell in the middle of the night, and had to traipse downstairs to the front door of his building. There was some total weirdo looking at him through the glass like *I'm here!* and Lamb recoiled—he had no idea who this tweaker was, but the dude started yelling at him, banging on the door to be let in, and then he actually put his hand through the glass and cut himself.

Blood everywhere, neighbors popping their head out their doors to see what the fuck was going on—the guy took off, but of course Lamb had to explain he didn't know who the guy was, and the old Mexican lady on the first floor made him clean up the glass and blood at three o'clock in the morning like it was his fault or something, while she stood frowning at the top of the stairs with one of her thin brown cigarillos, smoking and supervising.

Anyway, he called and told me about all this the next day at work, and I was like, "Are you *sure* you didn't call 976-GOTSEX and change your mind when you saw what he looked like?"

He insisted he didn't, and then he mentioned how he

remembered another time, back in college, when Arthur and Darla had called one of those numbers and given out the address of a "friend" who pissed them off—the poor guy was up answering the door half the night fending off horny randos.

BUCK

Pretty sure I mentioned how my whole dive back into Lamb's boxes and journals started because Fugie was bragging about having a stalker back in the day, this guy named Buck (real name Henry, I guess I can understand why he changed it.) Somehow Fugie insinuated himself into my group of friends all these years later, even though I've always found him pretty irritating.

He's the kind of guy who will tell you all about "my friend so-and-so" while you're thinking to yourself "I introduced you to so-and-so, dumbass," or casually mention that he spent $2,000 on a pair of sunglasses—you know it's a lie, but you also know that he thinks it makes him look good, even though the truth is that anyone who spends that much money on a pair of sunglasses is an idiot, so his lie actually makes him look like a fool twice over. Like I said, irritating.

Anyway, we were all out to dinner one night, and Fugie

pipes up about his supposed stalker, Buck, who just wouldn't take the hint, just wouldn't leave him alone, me me me, when the real headline was much worse. Honestly, I don't know how Fugie and Buck met, or how long it went on—he was shady about the details, so it could be that he did feel uncomfortable with the attention or whatever.

He definitely heard what happened between Buck and Lamb later on, but since that next chapter didn't revolve around Fugie himself, I guess it was unimportant. What I know is what I saw firsthand, and what Lamb told me later of course.

I wasn't there at Colossus when Fugie first introduced Buck and Lamb, it was brief, I think, and since Lamb was afraid of his own shadow, he never would have made eyes at a guy he thought was dating a friend. But he did tell me about this super hot guy that he met out dancing, and then of course, I met him myself when we went to a house party and Fugie brought Buck along with him.

There was definitely a veneer of sexiness. Buck had a rough-and-tumble look about him, punk-leaning, thick, very tan, blond crew cut, tattoos, Southern accent, devilish smile. OK, but let's be honest, he looked a little rednecky. On first glance, I wouldn't have minded a roll in the hay with him, but obviously when we met at that party, he was with Fugie—except that he wasn't, it turned out. I'm sure he could see that Lamb was all goo-goo over him, even though I was trying to keep Lamb distracted and chatting him up with other people.

Later on that night, while I was tongue-deep down this boy's throat on the sofa, there was a kerfuffle in the hallway with Fugie and Buck. I don't think it was heated really, but basically, Buck finally demanded to know where things were headed, and when Fugie said, "Nowhere," Buck grabbed Lamb and off they went—back to Buck's place.

Buck was a bit older than us, early thirties I think, and we were what, twenty-four? He had an apartment by himself up behind Dolores Park, and he had a car—he was a hairdresser over at the top of Solano, technically North Berkeley, so he made decent money from the biddies in the Berkeley Hills and Kensington, although Lamb found out he had massive credit card debt. (That would have been strikes one, two, and three in my book.)

What was I just saying about the veneer? The tan: tanning beds. The blond crewcut: bleached. The car: leased. The dazzling smile: actual veneers. Now I'm not saying these are bad things per se, but it is a little rich that Buck took Lamb with him to the Union Square Macy's one day to buy a suit, and after they stopped in a bar for a few cocktails, started loudly dissing a woman outside on the sidewalk for being fake with her hair and nails and facelift and fur coat.

So that was pretty nasty, but I guess Lamb calmed him down and kept it from turning into a full-on incident. You can probably see what was really at the bottom of all this: turns out, Buck was a raging alcoholic. (Sensing a theme in Lamb's taste in men, yet?) So there was that hanging over all their proceedings—and we're not talking beer and wine, but hard alcohol the minute Lamb arrived at Buck's to hang out, whether it was morning, noon, or night.

I remember the one time I hung out with them on a Sunday, it was Pride weekend, so me and Lamb went over to Buck's around 10 a.m. and a couple of Buck's friends were going with us, too—this English chick from when he lived in London for five years, and her American boyfriend. They were already three sheets to the wind when we got there, and Buck mixed up a big batch of kamikazes and poured them into sippy cups for all of us to take to the parade.

Not gonna lie, we were all shit-faced before the parade even started, and somehow we ended up back in the Castro—did we take Muni? We must have, but I don't remember it.

What I do remember is that we stopped at a hot dog joint on 18th Street. Was it Top Dog? I've always remembered it was Top Dog, but now I'm not sure if they ever had a location outside of the East Bay. While we were waiting for our food, Lamb and Buck and English girl and friend all started seriously making out against the condiments.

I was the fifth wheel, so I'm just watching this happen and laughing my ass off—I wasn't going to stop this car crash for anything—because the sauces were all in these big pump bottles, and Lamb and the girl were bent over backwards against the pumps with their respective boyfriends on top of them, and ketchup and two kinds of mustard are slowly squirting down their backs and turning the whole scene into a bloody mess.

Some people are laughing, some are grumbling because they can't put stuff on their dogs, and finally the guys behind the counter yelled at them to knock it off and get out of the way, but the chick slipped in the ketchup and lands on her ass in the middle of the floor, and a minor riot ensued over their dumbfuckery. I'm guessing we got thrown out without our hot dogs because I don't remember anything after that, total blackout.

And this was just one time hanging out with them. As Lamb told it, this was par for the course every time they got together. I think it was the first time he started having regular blackouts, and waking up the next morning in Buck's bed, sticky and naked.

"What'd you guys do this weekend?" I'd ask him, and he kept saying, "I don't know, but it must have been fun."

I was a little bit worried they might be having unprotected sex, and that he was getting so wasted every time they got together. I asked him if they had talked about HIV status, and Lamb said that Buck just told him I'm OK which didn't sound like a resounding no to me. But I think it did make him start to worry that he was getting in over his head with the drinking, and some of the other nasty shit that Buck was doing—not that Lamb could remember half of it, but there was an overall impression forming.

For one thing, it turned out that English chick and Buck used to do heroin together back in London. Was he actually clean? Anybody's guess.

For another, one night Lamb says to me, "Have you ever heard of this artist?" and gave me a name, I don't remember what. I hadn't ever heard of him, and this was all before the internet, so it's not like we could look it up.

"Well, it was the weirdest thing," he went on, "he made a big point of showing me this book he had that was all these paintings by this artist, but they were really weird— like all these old people sitting around a picnic table, staring up at a little girl standing on the table with her dress torn, and it was too short so you could almost see her bits, you know? Or other ones with people sneaking into nurseries in the dark, and kids huddled under blankets all scared with tears running down their faces. Nothing actually sexual, but really, really dark."

My blood ran cold when he told me that. I asked him what he thought about it, and he said he didn't know. "Was he trying to tell me something?" Honestly, I said, whichever way that might unfold, he was better off ending things sooner rather than later.

Eventually, Buck let loose with the n-word one night, and Lamb decided he'd had enough. He wanted to be brave and tell Buck face-to-face instead of over the phone. He went over, and I guess Buck was in a bad mood already because his friend had just gone back to London earlier in the day. When Lamb told him that he didn't want to see him anymore because he was turning into an alcoholic, Buck hit the roof. He started punching Lamb, gave him a black eye and a fat lip, and Lamb made a break for it. At the bottom of the stairs outside of his apartment, Buck yells down after him, "Enjoy the AIDS I gave you, faggot!"

So we had a thrilling six months waiting to find out if Lamb had HIV, which in the end he didn't—I wouldn't be surprised if they were both so drunk that no sex ever actually was accomplished, but either way he got lucky. I did a quick internet search recently, just to see whatever happened to Buck, and sure enough, he died due to complications of HIV infection in 1999, so what, just about six years later?

Anyway, Lamb was traumatized for a good little while after that, and I tried to be there for him, but with Lamb it was always this pendulum swinging way too far one way or the other. Fugie conveniently forgot all of that, so you can understand why I got a bug up my ass after he started shooting his mouth off about his eighth grade-stalking bullshit.

HE SAID, HE SAID

Back in the 90s, there was this local gay zine called *Rock Bottom* with the tagline *Because you gotta start somewhere*. There was always a picture of a different hot guy's bare butt on the cover, and you could buy it at a handful of shops and bookstores around town. It came out quarterly, pretty regular for six or seven years, until one day it just stopped and it took awhile for people to say, "Hey, whatever happened to that zine … what was it called? Acres of Ass? Butts O'Plenty? Swamp Bottom?"

It wasn't porn, although one issue a year was devoted to erotica. It was a total homemade jobbie—photocopied pages, folded in half and stapled—but it sold for $10 and you really would see people reading it at Café Flore (Café Hairdo, we called it) or BrainWash, that laundromat/café South of Market.

Anyway, as far as I know, the only piece of writing Lamb ever had published was the attached short story titled

"Rubber and Glue" in *Rock Bottom* (Volume 4/Issue 2) in spring of 1996. The theme of that issue was "First Times"—basically, all stories about when guys lost their virginity. I found a copy of it in Lamb's papers, as well as the original draft in his notebook.

I didn't get the whole story at the time, it must have been late in our sophomore year in college, so we were 19 and weren't actually out yet. He did tell me about a guy named Elmer—I remember making fun of it, like as in 'a millionaire and a yacht' Elmer?—but I see now that wasn't really his name, and I'm wondering why Lamb never shared this story with me.

Ashamed, I guess—he carried shame around with him like a pair of Coke bottle-thick glasses as long as I knew him. Even when we went out to bars, or walking down the street, he couldn't see guys checking him out—it was almost embarrassing—guys we knew would confess to me that they had a huge crush on Lamb, but they thought he was stuck up or standoffish because he was too afraid to look people in the eye.

Well it was the opposite, of course, it was a deep, cringing fear—it almost always is insecurity, isn't it?

Anyway, I think they only dated about a month, and when I asked him later How's Elmer? at first he forgot he'd given me a fake name and didn't know who I was talking about, and then said he had invited him to come hang out in Berkeley—rather than Lamb always taking BART over to the City to see him—and the dude ghosted him.

A while back, at least fifteen years or so, I went to Lost Weekend, the video store that used to be on Valencia, and picked up a VHS tape with a collection of gay short films from the 90s. Standard fare—meet cutes and missed connections sort of stuff. The last film caught me off guard—it was titled "Punk!" and it was Lamb.

It started out with him fully dressed in his bomber jacket and lace up boots and pegged acid-wash jeans, slowly undressing. It was completely silent, lots of zoom shots back out to long shots, shots going up and then back down. He was taking direction from someone, the guy behind the camera, who was obviously savoring this long, slow striptease of this crazy-tall kid in a mohawk down to buck naked.

How could he not know how beautiful he was? How could I have missed it?

"Rubber and Glue"

Willam Broeder

He told me a lot of things.

"We're all whores. We're all johns." His theory was that because gay men would have sex with just about anyone, we were in a unique position because the people we want to have sex with are not worried about their reputations, or babies. He said it was like a frat party, only all the guests are guys—no girls allowed—so no one was worried about people thinking they were a slut.

More than that, he said the beautiful thing was that we paid for sex with sex, rather than money—that sex is our currency, and the more we spend, the more we get in return.

He said he thought it was unnatural that men should be with women, rather than with other men—that it was weird how straight men wanted to be enfolded in all these soft things, the perfume and the makeup and the lace and hair. It was more natural that we should be attracted to people that like the same things we do: cigars, boots, leather, Levi's, beards, and crewcuts.

If anything, being attracted to women made a man soft (he'd say, "You are what you eat—so don't eat pussy!") and that it made more sense to him that women should like other women.

He said he had sex with Jim Morrison back in the day, when they were both film students at UCLA before anyone heard of The Doors. That they dropped acid, and Jim wanted to try it all—fucking, sucking, top and bottom, he wanted his mind blown—but when they came down from their trip, Jim left without saying a word and the next time he saw him walking down the street in Venice, Jim ignored him.

He was at the Six Gallery on October 7, 1955, he said—he was just a kid, and his mom was friends with Jay DeFeo. They both taught art classes for kids in San Francisco, and his mom thought it was bullshit when Jay got fired for shoplifting cans of spray paint. He was the only kid there, hidden in a corner on the floor because his mom couldn't get a babysitter. Everyone was loaded. Jack Kerouac tripped over him at one point and yelled at him, but after Allen Ginsberg read "Howl" and everyone was hooting and hollering, Jack grabbed him and hugged him. Or so he said.

He kept telling these scientists at UCSF that he didn't want to be part of their study—he said he was immune to HIV, and the wonks doing research wanted to know why, because he'd never used rubbers, giving or taking dick, but he was still healthy and that I didn't need to worry about him, that he was probably the safest guy to fuck in all of San Francisco.

He taught me how to spike my hair up—he was one of the first punks, he said, and knew one of the guys in the Dead Kennedys. He thought I would look cool with a mohawk, so he sat me down in his kitchen and buzzed my hair on the sides, and then went to work with Aqua Net and Elmer's glue. He said I looked super hot.

He took a bunch of pictures of me, and then he said he wanted to make a short film, so we got super drunk and high, and spent a whole night filming and fucking. In the middle of everything, he said he wanted to take me down to Jackhammer and show me off. I said, "I can't get in, I don't have a fake ID," and he said not to worry, he knew all the bartenders. So we walked down, and I didn't get carded. We did a bunch of shots, and then in the back corner, he got down on his knees and started sucking me off right in front of everyone. A bunch of guys were touching and kissing me, and at one point, someone got down on the floor and knocked him out of the way to get at me. That pissed him off and he dragged me out of there and back to his place for more drinking and filming.

He showed me a tape of a Cocteau Twins video he said he produced.

We smoked a bunch of weed that he said was "opiumated." "What's that?" He said it was weed infused with opium and made the high more intense and a little hallucinogenic. I didn't really feel any different than smoking regular weed, and he said it's because my drug palate was unsophisticated, but he would teach me all the good ones: opium, mescaline, peyote, DMT, MDA. "What's that?" Like ecstasy, only better and stronger, he said—the good stuff—he knew a guy called The Medicine Man, a shaman who led clients on trips and stuff, and could get anything he wanted. He said the trick was to drink grapefruit juice, that it intensified the effects of almost any drug, that old people had to be careful what they had for breakfast because they were ODing on their heart meds and blood thinners after eating half a grapefruit, or after greyhounds at the country club.

He knew this guy up in Mendocino who he said had

barrels of cash buried all over his property from growing marijuana in the national forests, that he had gone up many times to harvest weed with him. He called him a "white witch," said that he wouldn't go out at night without a hat on so moonbeams couldn't control his mind, that he was deep into the teachings of Edgar Cayce, and had made a huge fortune in the 60s and 70s as a painter, then bought this ranch in the middle of the redwoods and never left. He showed me a Ming Dynasty vase this friend gave him, said that if there were ever a fire, that's the only thing he would grab because it was worth a quarter million.

We walked out of a movie in Emeryville, and low in the sky there was this great big blob just hovering silently over the train tracks by the parking lot. He got really excited, and said, "UFO!" but it was only a blimp.

I said, "I love you," but he didn't say it back.

PUMP HOUSE

My parents were big drinkers so they never missed the stray bottles I pinched from their liquor cabinet, or from the cases of wine they'd haul back from one of their many Napa Valley wine tasting tours. They formed a couples darts league that usually met at our house, and my dad hosted poker nights with the boys, so bottles of everything were always showing up, opened and then forgotten. One time I found three different open bottles of Smirnoff.

Dad and one of his buddies constructed a bar out of plywood and two-by-fours, and upholstered it in the same carpet we had on the floors from some leftover pieces. It was kooky as fuck, but when Mom sent out invitations for their parties—her notecards printed with *"Have a Drink with Don & Noreen"*—there were always a lot of enthusiastic RSVPs.

They even bought a disco ball for the living room, and a fog machine that Dad loved to set up under one of the armchairs to scare the shit out of some unsuspecting wife or other who was just relaxing until this contraption suddenly started hissing out smoke from between her legs, his version of a fart cushion.

"Whoopie!" he'd yell. It was a big hit.

Thanksgiving vacation junior year at Wolcott, I grabbed a bottle of wine for a post-holiday party of our own, me and Lamb out on my balcony after lights out the first night back. We were out there around eleven o'clock, smoking in the dark, waiting for our friend Adam to sneak up from downstairs after the housemaster checked all the rooms to make sure everyone was where they should be. Mr. Barth had already checked our rooms upstairs, so Lamb climbed around the screen dividing the balconies to come over to mine—we were right next door to each other that year, convenient.

I remember I had just cracked open my bottle. "Ahh! Screw caps!" I said, which made us both giggle a little too much. I took a big slug, we passed it back and forth, and I was sitting there in my director's chair with the bottle on my knee, cigarette in hand, when the door to my room opened. The air current from the room door pushed the unlocked balcony door open a crack, and I said *Finally!* to Adam as the curtains started rustling.

But it wasn't Adam who emerged—it was Mr. Barth! My heart almost stopped.

Mr. Barth was a young guy, an alumnus of Wolcott who came back to teach after college—too goody-goody for my taste with his Bible study group. He was my faculty advisor the year before but I switched to Mr. Maxwell the music teacher as soon as I could.

There he was, standing in my doorway, and me frozen with a bottle of wine on my lap, ciggie smoldering. Lamb quickly ditched his off the balcony, but I was skewered—no getting around it. Barth was actually smiling, like he was happy to have caught me.

"Put it out," he said, and I dropped my ciggie into the Coke can I was using as an ashtray and swirled it around until it hissed in the liquid. It was pretty full of butts already, but he didn't investigate it further.

"Give me the pack." I calmly set the bottle of wine down on the floor by my chair, handed him the pack of cigarettes, saying absolutely nothing but waiting for all hell to break loose. "What is this, the third time?" he asked, meaning me getting caught smoking. It was the fourth, actually, but I just nodded. Besides the drinking and the smoking, one of the only things my brother ever taught me was *Do not volunteer information.*

"We'll talk in the morning. Get back to your room, Broeder," he said to Lamb, who booked it back over the balcony into his room. And then, without another word, Barth left.

Whoa. I couldn't believe that in his excitement over catching me smoking, he had completely missed the open bottle of wine sitting on my lap. Forever after Barth would always give me this sly look like *What are you up to?* whenever I'd see him around campus, and I couldn't help but laugh about what a goob he was.

Of course, an hour later, we were back out on the balcony finishing off that bottle, the six-pack Lamb had brought, and smoking most of the pack that Lamb still had. Epic night.

Two month's detention. Basically, I couldn't leave campus for two months, no trips into town, no weekends at home, and work duty every Saturday after classes for three hours. Lamb only got two weeks for being out of his room after hours. Barth himself admitted the next day he should have smelled his breath because Lamb was also caught smoking with me two of the three previous times. Thank god he didn't or he would have smelled the wine we both swigged.

Anyway, work duty was over at the far side of campus clearing brush on the slopes of the canyon above the fire road, and around the pump house at the edge of the hill. This squat outbuilding housed the old industrial-sized pump and pipes which fed the reservoir and avocado orchards of the Wolcott Ranch, and also a series of fire hydrants dotted around campus. Wildfires were always a threat, and we were tasked with clearing out the scrub and grasses so the pumphouse wouldn't go up in flames and knock out the water supply for the fire department if they needed it.

It was way out past the soccer field and we could see anyone coming a mile away, so we took a lot of cigarette breaks out there too. Mr. Barth would usually come out at the beginning to check on our progress, and we had to check in with him when we finished. There was all this wild white sage growing everywhere, and its minty-woodsy smelling oil got all over our skin and clothes as we were working so he could never smell the cigarettes when we came back at the end—plus we hid a bottle of Scope out there.

"This is actually pretty cool," Lamb said one Saturday we were working. We were taking a break, it was warm for

December and I remember we were still in shorts and flip flops, pretty much the school uniform even in class until after Christmas break and the couple of cool, rainy months over the winter. We would end up sneaking out to the pump house frequently for the rest of that year and next, until Lamb had his breakdown and withdrew before graduation.

That day, he was straddling this stone wall attached to the pump house, and I was perched on the iron railing that ran along the edge of the hill and the sheer, rocky cliff below.

"Yeah, peaceful," I replied. "Are you going to keep coming out after your detention is up?" I had six weeks more than him, and I wasn't looking forward to spending it alone. "I'll bring Oreos." He chuckled and nodded, although I knew he would have come out anyway even if I didn't bribe him with cookies.

We lit another cigarette, and launched into one of our favorite games, coming up with names of a nightclub we'd open after we got out of college—not sure where, probably L.A. because we didn't know yet that we'd both end up in the Bay Area.

"Violent Void," I said, imagining a dim, strobe-lit space painted black, with chain-link fencing to create different areas and rooms.

"Yes!" Lamb said, "That would be cool. How about Brennavaccaro—?" He ran it all together fast, this name that sounded funny but I didn't quite catch it.

"What's that? Dutch?" I said, but he shook his head.

"No, that actress, Brenda Vaccaro—I like her name." We had watched *Zorro, The Gay Blade* with my parents on a long weekend to my house recently so I knew who he was talking about. Don and Noreen thought it was a fucking hoot, George Hamilton as "Bunny Wigglesworth" this flamer with a whip screaming and laughing while he's dealing out vigilante justice.

("He makes a convincing ... fruit," my mom said, with her familiar whisper-wince like she was embarrassed to even say it, like *they* might be lurking behind the sectional and take offense.)

The actress was funny, but I curled my lip. "I don't know about that—maybe just Vaccaro, that's kinda cool—or Wigglesworth."

"Wigglesworth!" Lamb liked that one, nodding enthusiastically.

I was just at that moment lighting a new cigarette off my old one, perched on top of the railing, when a thought jolted me—it was staring us in the face.

"Pump House!" I cried out, and choked on the smoke I inhaled.

I guess I didn't really have my foot hooked around the spoke of the railing, just the end of my flip flop and my toes, because right as I yelled and choked, all of a sudden my foot didn't have hold of anything and I lost my balance.

Everything tilted, I went over backwards and started sliding off the railing!

All that life flashing in front of your eyes stuff? Bullshit. When you're flipping over the railing at the top of a hundred foot cliff, your only thought is *My cigarette!* Stupid, but that's what ran through my head.

My legs caught the top of the railing behind my knees so there was a second when I could have probably stopped myself, but it took me another second to consciously drop my ciggie to save myself. It would have been too late.

Lamb never moved so fast as that day.

He jumped up, tripped and skinned his knee, but managed to grab hold of my legs in his arms and held on for dear life—mine!

Not kidding, I would have been split open like a melon on the boulders at the bottom of that fall, or skewered on the giant aloe plants growing all around them.

I wriggled around to get a good grip and pull myself back up, panting with adrenaline and relief. "Pump House," I said, clinging to the railing. I wasn't sure if he'd heard me, and I didn't want to forget it. So dumb.

"Pump House," he whispered, and we both dissolved in hysterical laughter at I'm not sure what exactly.

THE FIRE ROAD PART II

"Markensteiiiiin ... Markensteiiiiin!" It follows you wherever you go, on the bus to town, across the quad, chased out of Penny's.

You disappear. You're invisible—nothing to see here—cuckoo, cuckoo, no one home. You are a ghost drifting around campus.

"Markensteiiiiin..."

Even freshmen and other sophomores chime in once the chanting starts.

Matt drinks it up. It feeds his rage, this poison. His hatred grows. The whole school is full of them—privileged bastards taught by fathers and brothers how to posture. How to stake their position at the top of the hill.

His own brother, Terry, had hated their kind. Used to tell him what a pack of jerks they all were and how glad he was to graduate and get the hell away from Buckley. But Matt doesn't want to think about Terry. Doesn't want to talk about Terry. He barely responds with a nod when he finally admits what happened, and you tell him how sorry you are.

It makes him seethe to see you treated this way. He can't be at your side every minute of the day. He wants to get back at them for every shitty thing.

"Who can summarize for me the first of Martin Luther's ninety-five theses?"

You watch as first one then another biffs the answer. Mr. Stalling clucks his tongue or stares up at the ceiling. He puts his hands behind his head. His armpits are sweaty. Finally, he cuts Dell off mid-sentence.

"Mr. Stern?"

You're startled. You stammer. "Sir?"

"Your thoughts on Luther's first thesis."

"Well..." You know the material. You studied with Matt the night before. He talked about the whole evangelical movement, Billy Graham and all that shit. "The first thesis set the groundwork for the shift from a relationship with the Church to a direct relationship with God," you begin, "but also set the wheels in motion for a fragmentation of Christian belief that doesn't really take into account..." You hesitate.

"Yes?" Mr. Stalling squints at you.

"It's just ... it lets anyone decide for themselves what's right or wrong—which is great if you are a kind, compassionate person, but if you are egotistical, you can talk yourself into believing anything is good, or anything is bad, without having to answer to anyone..."

"No. Mr. Stern. You need to demonstrate an understanding of the basic precepts before you start espousing opinions. Read from the book, please, Martin Luther's first thesis..." Thomas and his cohort snicker with glee at your discomfort. Your voice cracks as you read the passage. Mr. Stalling put his hands behind his head again. He closes his eyes and leans back in his chair.

Matt says Stalling is a weirdo. He's head coach of varsity lacrosse, has a sick fascination for Thomas and some of the other hot guys. That's just what he calls them: hot. Surprise, surprise—some boy's school teacher is storing up pictures in his head for a wank bank in his apartment later. But Thomas and the others eat up the attention and the accolades. If they don't spend too much time studying, they make up for it by hanging off of the coach on the sidelines.

"There will be a quiz on the reading next week—if, in fact, you do the reading, you should all get A's," Mr. Stalling says. There is a fair amount of grumbling. The weekend is now spoiled. The five quizzes make up twenty-five percent of the final grade for the semester. Mr. Stalling has a policy: the worst quiz grade will be dropped each semester. If you get four A's and an F, you can drop the F and still get an A.

"What are you doing after class?" Matt asks you. The bus starts running down to town at eleven for anyone who has a free last period. You are alone as you walk through the oaks on the way to Baker House.

You take a beat too long to answer. Your mind is elsewhere. "I don't know."

"Let's go explore," Matt says. "You've lived up here all

your life. Show me the sights."

You tell him you're really not up for it, but he insists. He wants to get a look all around the hill. Not just the campus area. He's already poked around and seen pretty much all of it, even went into some of the other dorms and looked around. He gets a thrill out of wandering around places he technically isn't supposed to be. Not that there's anything wrong with being in the common areas of a dorm. You know how when you see a kid from another dorm walking around in yours, you notice. They're out of place. You assume they are there to visit a friend or what have you. That's the look people give him, and he just stares right back, daring them to call him out. If he is blatant about it, like he owns the place, they never say anything. He once went into Mr. Perez's apartment when he wasn't there—didn't take anything, just looked around. You're not sure you believe him. He gets this look on his face in Spanish class sometimes. You see the way he looks at Perez.

Finally you agree to take him to the secret, off-limits places around the hill. There really isn't that much to see. Five hundred acres of avocados. A reservoir. The fire road that runs from the main road to town up through the canyons to the backcountry. He is interested in the ranch workers. He sees them around campus doing landscaping for the school, double duty with the ranch and Wolcott. They mow the lawns and trim the olive trees lining the quad. They rake up the olives messing the brick paths with their black mush. He noticed you say Hi to them and call them by name. Most of the snots on campus won't even look at them. You've known them all your life. They always treat you square.

You want to stop by your house and drop off your books and laundry first. He is cool with that. He helps you carry your laundry bag. Your mom is talking on the phone and just waves as you go in the back door. You take him upstairs to your room.

He is curious about all your stuff. He notices the holes in the walls where posters are missing, taken to your dorm room. "Let me guess: that's where Cyndi Lauper went. And that's Madonna."

He studies the books in your bookcase. "You've got a great collection," he says. He takes out your leather-bound boxed set of The Lord of the Rings. You've hardly touched it yourself. You don't want to mess it up. He opens up each volume and you hear the faint creak of the spines. You don't say anything. You don't want him to think you're fussy about stuff. He needs to touch everything. He picks up a Transformer from your bedside table. Puts it down on your desk. Flips back the blanket at the end of your bed. Doesn't flip it back down flat. He needs to leave his mark on things.

You tell him to wait there while you start a load of laundry. Your mom is still on the phone. When you get back up he's leaning up against your window jamb, staring out. The rolling crests of the trees stretch out to the hills, up and over into Los Padres, the national forest that borders your land.

"What's up there?" he asks. You tell him about the trails. The freshmen are taken up there on a ten-mile hike for Field Day every year. He missed it since he started as a sophomore.

You leave through the front door facing away from the

school. You walk out the main access road cutting across the orchards, the only one paved with asphalt. Others are just narrow dirt paths crisscrossing off of there for the trucks with equipment and for harvesting. There really isn't that much to see. You've been out there a million times. You help your dad sometimes. Pick avocados with the workers.

You lead him up toward the reservoir. It's a very large pond where water is stored for irrigation. There is a small outbuilding he seems interested in. He wants to climb over the chain-link fence to take a closer look, but the gate isn't even locked. Your dad lost the key and cut the padlock off with his bolt cutters. The pump house is locked though. You can't go in. He seems disappointed. "You think the key's back at your house?" You tell him it's probably on the key ring your dad carries around with him.

From there you make your way down the main road to the back canyon where it meets up with the fire road. He isn't interested in what's beyond there. It's mostly wide-open space for miles up and over the coastal hills. Lots of scrub—manzanita and sage—and rocks. He wants to follow the fire road back around the side of the hill. You squeeze through a chink in the gate and turn north toward the mouth of the canyon and the road to town.

Matt keeps bumping into you. He doesn't have a steady gait. He swoops and swerves, picking up sticks and looking around. He brushes up against you, or bumps into you from behind as he catches up. You suggest cutting up through a gully on the other side of the chain link fence. There's a pond surrounded by quicksand.

"Quicksand!" He's captivated. One of those things all kids know to fear: killer bees, Bigfoot, the Bermuda

Triangle, and quicksand. You throw a couple of big rocks into a slimy patch in the middle. They start to sink. You'll be waiting around all day to see them completely submerged. Up the middle of the gully, a path leads to a patch of gnarly old trees and the pet graveyard, dogs and cats from generations gone by. The trees are huge, old and unproductive, but your family keeps this little grove because carved into the trunks of them are old love notes. *Adam + Elanor* in a big heart, twenty years old by now. Their embarrassing love. Matt lays his hand on the tree. "Old man avocado."

To one side, the path branches off. You emerge from the orchard at the far side of the soccer field. You follow this below the lip of the hill under the eucalyptus trees. Paths crisscross the canyon for workers and students on detention to clear brush. You see down to the base of the hill to the shingled groundskeeper's cottage. Penny and her husband Ned live by the side of the fire road where it meets the main road.

You arrive at the other pump house, the big one which pumps county water up the hill to the reservoir and the school. This is where the heavy lifting happens. Matt wants to get into this one as well. There's a padlock on the door. You sit for a while on the far side against the cinder block wall. The hill falls off into a rocky precipice. You can see the ocean. You dangle your legs through the iron railing along the cliff edge.

"Want a cigarette?" He has them already in his hand. He pulls one out and lights it. "Marlboro Reds." You take one and he lights it for you.

"So what are we going to do about Thomas?" he asks.

You're caught off guard. You didn't know there was anything to do. Try to avoid him as much as possible and endure his teasing when you can't. Matt has other ideas.

"There's always something you can do."

Three weeks later, there's a pop quiz. History. No warning.

"If you've done the reading, you won't have any trouble answering these three questions," Mr. Stalling says.

You didn't do the reading.

He raises the pull-down projector screen to reveal what is written on the board. You have no clue. The Peace of Augsburg? You have to leave your page completely blank. Just your name and date at the top. Mr. Stalling looks through the answers as he collects them. When he gets to yours, he stops and stares at you.

"Didn't do the reading, Stern?" His eyes bore into you. He hates you.

"No. I—"

"Doesn't matter why. Automatic zero." He turns and shuffles the rest of the way down the line of desks.

Matt pipes up. "Mr. Stalling, is the worst quiz grade automatically dropped, or do we have to ask you for it?"

Stalling glares at him, then back at me. "Actually, it's at my discretion. Mr. Stern's blatant disregard for the reading assignment, for example, would not qualify."

Your mouth falls open. Sitting across from you, Thomas lets out a loud "Ha!" He delights in this game of gotcha. Your ears burn. There's nothing to do except keep quiet for the rest of class. He changed the rules on you. He's disliked you from the start. Maybe Thomas or the other boys on his lacrosse team have said things.

After class, you stay behind to speak to him. You apologize. You ask if you can do extra credit to make up for the zero.

"Three pages on the dissolution of English monasteries." He growls it without looking at you. He is irritated to even have to speak to you at this point. Matt is waiting for you outside the classroom door. You walk down the portico toward the old library. There is a set of encyclopedias. You want to see what they have to say.

"What a dick." Matt is furious. The treachery. Changing his own rules. He saw Stalling smile and chuckle when Thomas laughed. Stalling is playing up to his favorite student in some twisted reversal. "Thomas's pet teacher."

"It's done," you say. "I'll do the extra credit and try to stay on top of the reading for the rest of the semester. Maybe I can get transferred out of his section in the spring."

"How can we nail him?"

You don't put that much effort into your extra credit report. You feel stung. Stalling gave you no real direction. You decide he just wants to see that you've read and absorbed the subject. You paraphrase the encyclopedia entry and add some references to perspectives you find in another book. It is exactly three pages. You cite the two sources at the end. You leave it in Stalling's box outside the teacher's lounge on Monday morning. Even though he hasn't said so, you figure the extra credit will negate the zero on the pop quiz. They will cancel each other out.

At the beginning of the next class, Stalling makes a point of telling you in front of everyone to see him after class. For the next hour, Thomas sits smirking at you. He thinks you're in trouble. You can't imagine why. Thomas lingers after class but Stalling dismisses him. He shuts the door. You can still see Matt standing outside peeking through the glass. He gives you a little fist in the air.

"Mr. Stern." Stalling pulls your paper out from his book and drops it on the edge of his desk. There is a great red letter *F* written at the top. Your stomach drops. "You've managed to dig yourself an even deeper hole. At this rate, you'll fail my class this semester, which is unprecedented. You really just don't seem to give a shit."

You are shocked that he cussed. But you manage to protest. "I do care—I don't understand..." Your voice shakes.

"You're lucky I don't report you for plagiarism—but if you keep this up, I will." Stalling glowers at you. Now you really are baffled

"I didn't plagiarize."

"Bullshit." He spits it out with contempt. You aren't sure if you should press him. It isn't fair.

"I cited my two sources—I wrote three pages. I summarized the acts and issues and key figures—I didn't copy."

"Not word for word, maybe." He gets red in the face. "But I looked up your two citations, and you basically just restated what the encyclopedia said with a few notes lifted from the other source. What was your thesis?"

"Thesis?"

"Your analysis—your view on the subject? There wasn't a single original thought in this. You vomited back the information that you read with the words rearranged. You plagiarized!"

"I paraphrased." You are feeling more defiant. He never said anything about a thesis or analysis.

He is clearly getting hot under the collar and comes around the desk at you. "You plagiarized, goddammit! And you're going to admit it to me or I'm going to throw you up against that wall!" He knocks the paper out of your hand before sticking his finger in your face. "Admit it!"

"I can't admit something I haven't done!"

"Liar!" Stalling grabs you by your shirt and shoves you up against the chalkboard hard. Your head bangs it. You are so shocked you don't resist. The tears are coming. You feel small and powerless. "Admit it!" he repeats.

The door opens. You both turn your heads. Stalling immediately lets go of you and takes a step back. Matt stands in the doorway. His face is screwed up in a snarl like he is going to charge at Stalling. You grab your books and run out the door. Matt follows behind as you jog back to your dorm.

"I can't believe it! What are you going to do? Let's go talk to the dean!"

"No!" You round the corner into the hallway. "Let me think—I need to think about this..." Matt follows you right into your room and slams the door behind you.

"There's no thinking! We have to do something about him. He's got it in for you. He's out of control!"

"Who's going to believe me?" You are frozen at the door to your balcony looking back toward the history classroom across the quad.

"You have a witness—I saw the whole thing through the window."

You are too freaked out to say anything more about it.

He goes away grumbling.

You tell your mom what happened. Maybe it's a mistake. You never see Mr. Stalling again. Mr. Hutchins steps in for the rest of the semester. It's nearly Christmas break anyway. They tell everyone that Mr. Stalling has a family emergency and needs to take a leave of absence. Word gets around that you squealed on him for yelling at you. Maybe Stalling told his favorites it was your fault he was being dismissed without the important part where he laid hands on you.

Everything gets much worse after that. The Markenstein catcalls are almost constant. You know your mom was just trying to protect you, but it's turned Thomas and crew mean. They shoot spitballs at you, steal your blanket off your bed and shove it in the toilet. They spread the rumor that you offered to suck Stalling off for a better grade and that's why he got in your face and got fired. It's becoming intolerable. You start to spend nights at home. You are effectively a day student again. Matt isn't happy about it. He hates everyone but you.

"What can we do?" you say. He gets this knowing look on his face.

The Thursday before Christmas, everyone is leaving to go home after class the next day. You're walking up the road past the dining hall, over by the backyard where they keep the dumpsters. It's the first really cold day of the year. You are hunkered down in your coat, cap on, hands shoved deep in your pockets. The smell of the garbage wafts through the gate as you walk past. You are distracted, trying to get to class on time.

"Markensteiiiiiin!" Someone growls from inside the yard.

You turn. Out of nowhere, a sharp object punches you in the eye. Pain explodes like you've been stabbed.

You scream. You can't see anything. Your whole face is slimed, something wet and crunchy. The searing sharpness of it doesn't subside. You are on your knees on the ground, completely blind. Eventually you hear footsteps and Spanish. The kitchen crew comes out to see what's going on. You are led blind to the infirmary, which is right next to the dining hall.

The nurse doesn't even wait for an ambulance. She throws you in her own car and drives you to the emergency room in town. It was an egg. It hit you straight in the eye. The shell perforated your eyeball and tore it open. They give you a shot that blurs everything out. A week before Christmas, you have surgery to repair a ruptured cornea. You have stitches in your actual eyeball.

The dean comes to the hospital and asks you a bunch of questions. The police even come and take a statement. You aren't able to tell them much. It was like you'd been struck by lightning. They press you on the voice that called out, but it was that monster-voice they all put on when they moan at you. It could have been anyone. At least you know better than to point the finger at Thomas or any of those guys. When the bandage comes off, your eyesight is blurry and dark. You have to wear an eyepatch.

Your mom is reluctant to send you back, even as a day student. You have to convince her. At least the taunting stops after school starts again.

Matt is incensed. He comes straight down to your house

when he gets back to campus. He commiserates with you. What a bunch of animals they all are. They deserve whatever is coming to them.

"An eye for an eye," he says. "No, seriously. You might never see right out of that eye again, and no one gets punished? We know who did it."

"We don't know for sure," you say. But he isn't happy about it.

SUNDAY MORNING

Sunday morning on the phone 1989

Me (italics): Hello?

Lamb (bold): Hey it's me.

M: Hey me.

L: I can't believe you're awake.

M: I'm not.

L: Sorry. You go out last night?

M: No, but I was up until two watching a movie.

L: What movie?

M: The Shining.

L: No.

M: Yes.

L: It's so scary!

M: Aww, you and your scary movies—well it's not your typical scary, except for maybe the one actual ax murder. And a little blood...

L: No thanks.

M: You liked Rosemary's Baby...

L: That was eerie, not scary. Eerie is fine.

M: Rosemary's other baby. Anyway, what's so important at the crack of crack you gotta call me before I've even had my first cigarette—in fact, hold on ... [lights cigarette] ... right then—spill it.

L: I fucked up.

M: Tell me.

L: So my roommate found my stash of porn and kinda freaked out on me.

M: Ernie? OK—where was it?

L: In my bottom drawer, but I accidentally left it open and he saw the mags, and...

M: And what?

L: And I had a pair of his underwear in there too.

M: Oh. What were you doing with it—were you...?

L: No I wasn't sniffing it, I ran out of clean underwear and I borrowed a pair.

M: Fuck sake, why didn't you just go commando?

L: Well...

M: What now?

L: It's just I didn't have time to shower, and well...

M: Well what?! Fuck sake, spit it out, man!

L: It's just that I'm really hairy and it's hard to keep my butt clean after I poop, I wipe and wipe and it just never gets totally clean, so all my underwear was ... you know ... and I didn't want to get my pants dirty.

M: Jesus. Thanks for the visual. So you've got a skid mark problem, and you decided better his underwear than your pants. Can't say I blame him for getting mad.

L: Well he doesn't know any of that—I already washed them, but when I folded my laundry I accidentally put them in my drawer with all of mine instead of putting them back in his and so he probably does think I was sniffing them or something. Anyway, it was more than just mad—he got really mean, said I was sick and I'm pretty sure he told Tessa and Mark because now no one will sit with me in the dining hall, and they all just ignore me.

M: Oh, well that's not cool. But you know what, he's no prince—he gives a really toothy blow job.

L: What?

M: I didn't tell you because he was such a freak about it but yeah we fooled around that Saturday morning you had to work last time I came up.

L: Oh my god, he's gay? What do you mean toothy?

M: Like teeth marks on my dick for two days toothy! And then he said he'd kill me if I told anyone, which was a crock of shit obviously, but I was so like, ugh gross, I can't believe I fooled around with this jerk, and then I didn't tell you because I didn't want things to get weird between you, but you took care of that, so. Now what?

L: I asked him if he was going to move out, he's hardly ever here anyway—he goes home

most weekends to see his girlfriend...

M: *Ha! Lucky girl.*

L: **Anyway, he said "No, why should I?" but he was really pissed and he won't speak to me and I read in his journal he called me a "thing" and now no one else is talking to me either.**

M: *You read his journal too?! What the fuck, is nothing safe with you?*

L: **He left it open on his desk, like he wanted me to see it.**

M: *Oh, OK, well maybe he did. I don't know what to tell you. Have you learned your lesson at least? Are you going to borrow his underwear or read his journal anymore?*

L: **No.**

M: *Alright, well I say fuck 'em—fuck all of them—school's out in two months and you never have to see any of those dicks again.*

L: **I guess so.**

Sunday morning at 16th Street & Mission 1993

L: **Oh my god it's Ernie! Stop, he'll see me. Hide!**

M: *What? Where?*

L: **Walking across the street—right there.**

M: *Oh my god, wow, he looks rough. REALLY rough. What's that under his arm?*

L: **It's a rolled up sleeping bag.**

M: *Huh. Heading toward BART. He looks like a*

drug addict.

L: He came out of that SRO.

M: SRO?

L: One of those flop houses, you know, last stop before sleeping on the sidewalk.

M: He's gone—can we keep walking please? This alley smells like piss.

L: He did look rough. I wonder if he's using heroin.

M: Good bet. Why else would anyone come down to 16th Street with nothing but a sleeping bag to spend the night in a crack house?

L: Well I didn't say crack house.

M: Whatever. Was he doing heroin in the dorms?

L: No, but he was curious about it, and he was always hanging around Telegraph talking to the street kids. One time he brought a homeless dude upstairs to our room like 'haha look what I found' and the guy was asking for money to get to San Francisco so Ernie gave him a jar of pennies. I said, "Ernie, you have a car," and he looked at me like he was going to kill me.

M: Serves him right. Dumbass.

L: Anyway, he said to me, "Fine, but you're coming with us," so we all piled in his old Beetle, and then when we got to the Bay Bridge, Ernie says to the guy, "You got toll money?" because neither one of us did, and the dude starts counting out pennies from the jar we gave him!

M: No! Ha! I love it!

L: It took us ten minutes! People were pissed.

Sunday morning on BART 1995

L: Don't turn around.

M: What? Why? Who's there?

L: It's Ernie. OK actually I guess you can turn around, he's super out of it.

M: What's wrong with him? Why's his head back like that?

L: He must be high.

M: Whoa. It's bad. He looks bad. Oh my god, look at his arm!

L: What the fuck is that?

M: It's an abscess. Addicts get them from dirty needles.

L: Oh my god. Oh my god! It's huge, oh my god it looks like he was sliced open with a knife. Why isn't it bleeding? A needle didn't do that.

M: It does if your tracks get infected and you don't have it treated—it's an open wound, but it's old—festered and dried up. He must have had it for awhile.

L: I think I see bone!

M: Stop! Don't look. Ignore him. Ugh. Poor guy. He's going to die. Wow.

L: He's getting up.

M: What?

L: He's getting up—he's getting off the train. He's puking on the platform!

M: Jesus. Jesus!

ROOM FOR DESSERT

By the time he was twenty-eight, Lamb still had never had a real boyfriend—that is, someone who lasted more than a month, at least long enough to say *I love you* and mean it. I think he was starting to feel like there was something wrong with him, even though I tried to tell him that it didn't mean anything.

I was still single too, although I'd dated a couple guys—one for about six months, and another for about a year—Mikey. He was a waiter up in Mill Valley at some swank restaurant, sexy as hell, and we did fall into a sort of comfortable rhythm of weekends and sleeping over, even took a trip to Puerto Vallarta together.

Funny—I think it was the *I love you* that did us in. We tried it on for size, and realized it was a bad fit almost immediately. He liked to call me *Wall Street* because I worked on Montgomery downtown—Wall Street West—I think he looked down on my career ambitions, confusing my need to be gainfully employed with some sort of moral failure.

"Capitalist." That's the last word he threw at me over the phone when we broke up, not even in anger, just some weird dismissal he needed to put me behind him.

Anyway, I said to Lamb, "The best way to get into a good relationship is to stay out of a bad one," and I meant it, especially after all the funky near-misses he'd had—Elmer, Arthur, David the sleepy turtle boy, and of course, Buck the pedophile.

"Any red flags?" I'd ask him whenever he mentioned a new guy, and he would list them off, and I'd give him my song and dance. "You get what you settle for," I'd say, and he'd go off and things would fizzle.

So Randy. I guess you really can't blame someone else for your own problems, or in this case Lamb's, but it did seem like things went downhill during and after their relationship. Randy was much older than Lamb—twenty-one years older, so pushing fifty. I can't say he wasn't charming, and sort of cute in a chubby Tom Selleck kinda way. Tall too, I think that was one of the attractions because he was almost as tall as Lamb, maybe taller since Lamb had such a terrible slouch.

They met at The Club, the bar where Lamb worked, on a quiet night mid-week when it was mostly empty, and Lamb was glad to have someone who actually wanted to sit and talk with him for an hour or two. It happened fast, as I recall, like they started dating one minute, and the next, Lamb said he was moving in with Randy in this little in-law cottage he was renting behind a Victorian on Duboce Park.

They had that European connection in common: Randy went to boarding school in Switzerland. He was the son of some hotshot shipping executive with Aristotle Onassis's company back in the day. Randy implied his mom and dad had been friends with Ari and Jackie O, that he met them briefly once at a party on a yacht when they went on vacation in Greece.

Whatever glory days he once had with his parents were long over, though—his dad dropped dead of a heart attack in the seventies and left his mom with massive debts. Anyway, Randy lived in London for a long time working in a variety of galleries, which is how he came to have this odd collection of art and furniture—lots of mid-century stuff, Noguchi this and Heywood Wakefield that, a Clarice Cliff dinner set, and all these other little gewgaws.

It was one night when they invited me over for dinner so me and Randy could get to know each other a bit better that I first started having some real worries about Lamb. I mean, he worked at a bar after all, and I never heard of him getting into trouble, getting drunk at work or whatever, but that night at the *Fairy Cottage* (Randy called it) was a trip.

First of all, it started off with Happy Hour, which is a funny sort of thing to call drinks before dinner at your own house, but it really was a solid hour of gin and tonics—like, I had to say *no* to the fourth one I was offered because I was getting hammered, and Randy had five bottles of wine set up on his fancy blond wood sideboard "breathing" before dinner so I knew it was going to be a whole thing. He was a fantastic cook, actually, no problem there—Lamb was definitely eating well with his new boyfriend—but there were other things.

For one thing: "*COCKTAIL* table!" Randy corrected Lamb like three times when he said *coffee table* including one time when I was the one who said it, but he admonished Lamb like we were a single uncouth unit.

Lamb had a new haircut, pretty conservative standard-issue, and no crazy colors or anything. Also, he had a whole new wardrobe, seemed like—and that night he was wearing a sweater, which I'd literally never seen him wear before in my life. We used to joke about sweater queens in a *Kill me if you ever see me in a cardigan* kinda way, and don't even get me started about the car coat Randy picked out for him, like something your mom puts on to go to the grocery store.

And then there were the Italian shoes, these super narrow, pointy-tipped jobbies that Randy actually called out.

"How do you like my boy's new shoes?" he asked as we were drunkenly melting into the giant kidney-shaped white sofa, and before I could answer, added, "I finally convinced him to spend more than fifty dollars on a pair of shoes."

$400, Lamb confessed when I asked him about all this later.

"Do you have that kind of money to throw at shoes?" Not really, apparently—he was running up some hefty credit card bills of his own since they'd gotten together. Bearing in mind that he had been wearing combat boots from the Army Surplus on Market Street since college days, this was a pretty drastic change.

Dinner was all candlelight, linen tablecloth and napkins,

and this enormous arrangement of hydrangeas big as a beachball that Randy refused to move because "It's just so pretty!" I couldn't really even see Lamb on the other side of the table and it ended up just Randy talking at me through the whole meal because we were sitting across from each other. At some point Lamb actually moved his chair around the corner of the table so we could see each other, which solved the problem but how strange.

The oddest moment of the evening, though, came after dinner—and yes, we went through all five bottles, a specific one for each of the courses—when Randy started marching me around the house to explain all his collectibles and art.

There was the red-headed French showgirl leering down from over their bed, some vintage Art Nouveau poster he found at a Paris flea market. The Miró lithograph. The Liberty sterling candle sconce. The Wiener Werkstätte chess set. Nothing especially valuable, but all of it *precious* if you get my drift.

The finale, though, was this enormous painting taking up an entire living room wall—it wasn't a big wall, but it was a big painting—and that's when Lamb, hanging in the background as I'm being grand-toured around the house, disappeared into the bedroom. I sort of stopped and turned toward the bedroom door expecting him to reappear and rejoin the lecture, and Randy physically took me by the elbow and steered me back to stand in front of the painting to hear his spiel.

He dropped some German artist's name—"Jewish, surrealist, an acolyte of Chagall's, he met him in Berlin when Chagall exhibited there"—and emphasized how he spent every dime he had and ate Campbell's soup for three months after he bought it. The gallery he worked for had secured the sale of a cache of the artist's paintings bricked up in a basement during World War II and only rediscovered in the 80s.

He went on like some kind of docent. "Notice the four figures, two men and two women—but no, just one man and one woman—through their own and each other's eyes. On the left, a cavalier as the man sees himself, caped and daring, but beside him, the clown, as the woman sees him. On the right, a great lady seated with her elegant fan as the woman sees herself, but behind her, the harlot, as the man sees her."

I'm not saying it wasn't a cool story, but by the time he finished, I was ready to keel over. And that's when Lamb came out of the bedroom, reeking of weed, and I was just ... puzzled, I guess. I mean, we smoked weed all the time, or used to anyway back in college, so it was really strange to me that he had stepped out of the room like he had to hide it or something. Or maybe Randy wasn't into it? I have no idea, but it was the first time it occurred to me that he was going down a darker path—like four or five cocktails, a couple bottles of wine, AND weed?

It was a lot, but it was the sneaking that stuck with me.

By the time Randy announced, "I made a Pavlova!" I was ready to puke.

Anyway, I'll just mention one other incident at the Christmas party they threw that year. I was in the kitchen talking to Randy when his friend Steve arrived and came in to say *Hi*. Super annoying dude with a lot of teeth wearing some crazy ass five-in-one Christmas sweater like he couldn't decide which one to wear so he wore them all.

He says to Randy, "And so—how's your not-so-little project coming along?"

Randy glanced at me so of course I instantly knew he was talking about Lamb.

"It's fine—great actually."

But his friend Steve was one of these dicks who likes to keep pushing buttons. "Miss Doolittle's responding to her education then?"

At that point I just turned and walked back out to the party.

They lasted just over a year. Lamb put on a fair bit of weight, but he was in love supposedly so he really was shook when he came home early from work one weeknight because the bar was slow and he wasn't feeling well. He walked in on Randy with some random dude's hand up his ass and a big pile of cocaine chopped up on the Noguchi glass COFFEE table.

THE BOX

When I look back on our last two years at Wolcott now, Lamb was like the canary in the coalmine of old school toxic masculine bullshit. Despite his height and presence, he was especially susceptible to the viciousness of school boys and endured almost daily bullying.

Some got it into their heads that his slow-motion way of walking, all knees and elbows, was a little swishy, so they would walk behind him in an exaggerated imitation to the general amusement of everyone.

And because he had what we call in the biz gay twang— that sort of nasally, lispy way of talking that marks some guys for ridicule—they would call out to him mockingly across the quad or in the dining hall. At first, he didn't realize these were pranks and thought he hadn't heard properly, would go over and ask them *Sorry, what did you say?* and when they laughed and he got mad, they'd ask what was his problem? I tried to stop him from engaging, but even though I told him to just ignore them and they'd eventually stop, I realized pretty quick that only worked if they didn't get a rise out of him.

But they did. Lamb was a furious blusher, and even once he got wise to what was going on and stopped reacting, they could still plainly see he was bright red with embarrassment, and that seemed to delight them even more.

At the center of all this, of course, was Thomas. Ever since their initial run-in sophomore year in the dining hall, Thomas had made it his unofficial career at Wolcott to find ways to humiliate Lamb at every turn, escalating after he caught Lamb that one time keeping guard outside Mr. Perez's apartment.

Because he didn't know I was there—yes, stealing booze, cigarettes, and weed—anytime something went missing in the dorm, Thomas immediately pointed the finger at Lamb. It became a general rumor that Lamb was a thief and couldn't be trusted, and yeah, I felt a little responsible for the reputation he got.

Sophomore year, Thomas had got in good with a bunch of junior and senior guys on the varsity teams because he was such a great athlete, and really, he could do no wrong with any of the alpha-dogs and was promoted into that good old boy gestapo immediately. Thomas's star only seemed to rise higher as he found ways to torture the less developed or less fortunate, anyone who stood out for all the wrong reasons really, and no one stood out more—by standing a foot taller than everyone else—than Lamb.

Our junior year, there was one senior, a sadistic fuck named Snyder, who adopted Thomas as his lieutenant in

Overton House where he was prefect. Lamb and I were in Short House, and we got along pretty well with everyone. Our senior prefect, Lanier, was usually pretty chill but we also tried to keep our illicit activities on the down low so as not to incur his wrath because he did have a temper on him.

So here's what happened from what I could gather from the kid who came down to my room at 6 a.m. the next morning, and in subsequent conversations over the ensuing days. Lamb would never talk to me about it, and he didn't write anything in his journals then or ever, as far as I can tell, though he did write that story that seems to enact some sort of revenge on Thomas. It's a bit freaky, and so unlike the Lamb I knew, but it does give some insight into how he ended up in rehab after assaulting one of his Daddies.

Anyway, this kid, I don't even remember his name, comes down to Short House and tells me I better get up to Overton common room and look in The Box. What the fuck are you talking about? I asked him, and he said that Lamb had gotten caught out of his dorm last night, and Snyder and Thomas had put him in the old fireplace woodbox in the common room.

"What are you saying?" I demanded.

"He's still in there."

So I raced to Overton just wearing the t-shirt and boxers I slept in, and there was the so-called box in a corner with a peg through the clasp. It was pretty big—about half the length of a coffin, maybe, but wide and fairly tall, almost waist-high—but nothing you'd want to spend the night in, that's for sure. Anyway, I went and opened it up, and Lamb was curled up inside, blinking, sheet-white, nearly catatonic. I had to smack his face a couple of times to get him to snap out of it, and then help him out. He was bent over almost double with stiffness, and I walked him back to our dorm. Luckily, no one was around to see all this—breakfast started at 6 a.m., so if you weren't up in the dining hall eating, you were still in bed before chores started at seven.

He wouldn't speak or look at me, just crawled in bed and pulled the covers up over his head. What happened? I kept asking, but he wouldn't respond, and I thought, well, he probably needs to just sleep it off and he'll be better by the afternoon.

What I gathered later from Lanier himself was that he'd caught Lamb smoking on his balcony and threatened to turn him in for something like his fifth offense, which probably would have gotten him suspended. He sent Lamb up to Overton around midnight on orders to bring back a copy of Penthouse from Snyder, which was just a bitch-ass way to punish Lamb without doing any of the dirty work himself.

Apparently, Overton common room was a free-for-all after lights out, with Snyder and Thomas conducting nightly rituals involving actual floggings with a paddle, time-outs in The Box sometimes two at a time if the boys would fit, and "thumpings"—basically a circle of guys standing around a victim, screaming and knocking him around like a mosh pit.

According to some others who'd been there, they thumped Lamb for a good while—a junior, thumped by freshmen and sophomores, and Thomas in his own year—

and then Thomas himself gave the order that Lamb should be put in The Box, and threatened anyone who let him out with the flogging of their life.

Anyway, that morning I told the dorm master that Lamb wasn't feeling well and needed to stay in bed for the day. By the end of classes, I found him up and at least able to nod his head yes or no again.

Problem was we had a recital the next day in English that we had all been working on for awhile. We had to recite from memory no less than 500 words from Moby-Dick, extra credit if you did 1000. We'd been memorizing and reciting it back to each other for weeks to get it right. I wasn't entirely sure Lamb was going to manage it. He refused to practice that last night beforehand, and went to bed early.

In English class next day, we went in order down the line, and when Lamb's turn came up, he stood and went to the front. Mr. Dunning didn't tolerate much nonsense in his class, so there wasn't much going on before Lamb started, but as he got going, all hell broke loose.

A sweet and unctuous duty! No wonder that in old times sperm was such a favourite cosmetic. Such a clearer! such a sweetener! such a softener! such a delicious mollifier! After having my hands in it for only a few minutes, my finger felt like eels, and began, as it were, to serpentine and spiralise...

I'd told him not to pick that piece; I knew he was going to take shit for it. But that was before The Box, and he'd been feeling bold. He said it spoke to him. He imagined it was his chance to strike one for Fellowship (he actually said that—who says shit like that?) and besides, it was also funny—everyone would have a good laugh. Oh boy.

... as I bathed my hands among those soft, gentle globules of infiltrated tissues, wove almost within the hour; as they broke to my fingers, and discharged all their opulence, like fully ripe grapes their wine; as I snuffed up that uncontaminated aroma, - literally and truly, like the smell of spring violets; I declare to you, that for the time I lived as in a musky meadow; I forgot all about our horrible oath; in that inexpressible sperm, I washed my hands and my heart of it...

By this time, the groans and guffaws really started to build. As he looked around he clearly realized he'd made a mistake, that he'd picked the piece in a moment of foolish optimism. But he couldn't stop now, our recitation counted half as much as the mid-term, and flubbing it could drop your final grade a point.

... Squeeze! squeeze! squeeze! all the morning long; I squeezed that sperm till I myself almost melted into it; I squeezed that sperm till a strange sort of insanity came over me, and I found myself unwittingly squeezing my co-labourers' hands in it, mistaking their hands for the gentle globules. Such an abounding, affectionate, friendly, loving feeling did this avocation beget; that at last I was continually squeezing their hands, and looking up into their eyes sentimentally, as much as to say, - Oh! my dear fellow

beings, why should we longer cherish any social acerbities, or know the slightest ill-humour or envy! Come; let us squeeze hands all round; nay let us all squeeze ourselves into each other; let us squeeze ourselves universally into the very milk and sperm of kindness.

By the end, Lamb barely squeaked out that last line, and even Mr. Dunning was openly laughing while Thomas and his posse were screaming with hilarity, shouting out offers for Lamb to get his hands on their sperm. It was a nightmare.

It took quite a while for the hysterics to die down. Finally, me next, I began my recitation, and I couldn't take my eyes off Lamb, folded in his seat like a caterpillar frozen in its cocoon, unseeing.

... But we are all in the hands of the Gods; and Pip jumped again. It was under very similar circumstances to the first performance; but this time, he did not breast out the line; and hence, when the whale started to run, Pip was left behind on the sea, like a hurried traveller's trunk. Alas!
I should have stopped him. I never should have let him pick that stupid passage; never should have got him smoking cigarettes in the first place for that matter.
... The intense concentration of self in the middle of such a heartless immensity, my God! Who can tell it? Mark, how when sailors in a dead calm bathe in the open sea—mark how closely they hug their ship and only coast along her sides...

I thought of him shut up in that chest, the shame he felt. I glanced at him again and almost lost my train of thought, his face drained of all color like the morning before. Lost.

... The sea had jeeringly kept his finite body up, but carried down alive to wondrous depths, where strange shapes of the unwarped primal world glided to and fro before his passive eyes; and the miser-merman, Wisdom, revealed his hoarded heaps; and among the joyous, heartless, ever-juvenile eternities, Pip saw the multitudinous, God-omnipresent, coral insects, that out of the firmament of the waters heaved the colossal orbs. He saw God's foot upon the treadle of the loom, and spoke it; and therefore his shipmates called him mad. So man's insanity is heaven's sense; and wandering from all mortal reason, man comes at last to that celestial thought, which, to reason, is absurd and frantic; and weal or woe, feels then uncompromised, indifferent as to his God.

BABY

After the debacle junior year with The Box, things seemed to calm down. Snyder, the senior dick who oversaw that whole operation, graduated along with a big chunk of the worst jocks, so Thomas lost most of his posse.

Generally, our class was known for being more level-headed and serious about academics, so Thomas didn't have any luck forming a new hit squad early senior year. Some of the younger boys who had tormented Lamb that night actually expressed some remorse to him later—a couple wrote apologies in his junior yearbook—so we were headed into senior year with relative peace except for one unfortunate detail.

Lamb and I had been in the same dorm sophomore and junior years, and Thomas had always been in a different one, but senior year on move-in day, who was already running all over Short House when we walked in the door with our trunks but the big man himself. Our pleas on our dorm request forms ("Pleasc, please, please Short House") had neglected to mention the other most critical factor in the room assignments ("...and not with Thomas!") Still, with senior year upon us and me to look out for him, I was pretty sure I could keep a lid on things. Even Thomas wasn't so cocky as to think he could get away with hazing another senior.

Truth be told, we didn't spend a lot of time in the dorm. Most Wednesday and Saturday half-days we were either down at the pump house smoking cigarettes and weed (by that time my brother was dealing out of his off-campus apartment at USC and we were well-supplied) or we'd take the shuttle into town and hang out at the beach, Denny's, or the movies. Sometimes we'd take weekends at my parents' house out in Lancaster, and during the winter we'd go skiing up at Mountain High, the little ski resort up in the San Gabriel Mountains that was only about an hour's drive away.

Night skiing was our favorite—we'd get super high in the car when we got there, and then head up to the top of this quiet, shadowy mountain. Not a lot of people, usually, we'd pretend we were super spies and go streaking down the slopes at top speed with hardly anyone else around. There was this one side trail through a clump of pine trees where we'd swoop up and down and around the trees and moguls. At a couple of spots you had to duck under low-hanging branches—dangerous, maybe, if you didn't know they were there, but we'd been so many times we could almost ski our secret run with our eyes closed.

Things were looking up, and when spring rolled around, Lamb got into every school he applied to—my parents pressured me to go to USC because that was where my dad and brother went and it was closest to home, so that was a done deal. Lamb had his choice of Harvard, Stanford, and USC, as well as all the UCs, but he hadn't made his decision yet when the whole business with Thomas finally came to a head.

There was this freshman kid named Polley in our dorm, so small and thin you were afraid to breathe next to him for fear you would blow him away, the very kid who early that year was coming up the stairs from his room as Lamb was going down and tripped over his own feet, landing in a heap on top of Polley and fracturing his wrist. Anyway, Lamb felt really bad, took the kid up to the infirmary and all that, and felt a little protective of him from then on.

Problem was that Polley was an easy mark for Thomas, who was looking for an outlet since his old crew had graduated and taken all their shenanigans with them. He was relentless with his harassment of this kid, mainly centered around this kooky comforter Polley had brought with him from home. It was this odd Native American pattern in pastel colors, like something you'd see upholstered on your hippie aunt's sofa, and it was the first thing you saw when you walked into his room.

Naturally, Thomas seized on it the first week of school as he was marking his territory in Short House, and I mean actually grabbed it off of Polley's bed and went running down the hall as everyone was standing around one afternoon before dinner.

"Look at this shit!" he yelled, waving it around like a flag. "What the fuck is this?! What a freak! Someone start a fire so we can sacrifice it to the goddess of homosexuality!"

Poor Polley was in tears his third day on campus, and for the rest of the year the gay blanket would be paraded around the dorm on a regular basis, and hidden in various spots just before lights out. Eventually Polley began to take it in stride, and always found it before bedtime, so the prank lost some of its power after a while. He also had proven himself such a nimble soccer player they made him co-captain of the JV team, and when he grew four inches before our eyes and his voice suddenly changed over Christmas vacation, we stopped worrying too much about him.

One fateful night in the spring, however, proved Lamb's unraveling. Thomas had stolen Polley's comforter for the umpteenth time, and hidden it in a new place—right under Polley's own bed, as it happens, but it was literally the last place he'd look because it had always been taken out of his room and stashed in any number of different places. Frustrated though he was, Polley refused to name Thomas as the culprit when Mr. Barth came around at lights out and found the poor kid shivering under just a sheet in his bed. It was a particularly chilly spring, and so Barth went around questioning everyone about the comforter until he got to Lamb.

He told me later he said to Barth, "Why don't you ask Thomas? He's the one who hid it—he's been doing it all year." I mean, points to Lamb for finally calling the bastard out knowing that there would be some kind of retaliation. Thomas got detention for his year-long course of harassment and acted like Lamb shouldn't have snitched, like he owed him a damn thing after everything he put him through? Fucking prick.

Anyway, about a week later the whole incident was all but forgotten by everyone except Thomas, apparently, because that's when he struck back one night after lights out. Thomas got suspended for two weeks, not that it mattered much because seniors had all pretty much checked out for the rest of the year anyway with college acceptances locked in regardless of what grades or other disciplinary matters might arise. I suppose if he'd actually been expelled it might have made a difference, but the prank he played on Lamb didn't really seem to warrant a stronger response despite the terrifying reaction Lamb had to it. He was obviously more on the edge than I or anyone realized.

So late one night, it must have been around 11:30 or so, me and Lamb were hanging out in my room. Seniors didn't have lights out, and only had to be in their dorms after the ten o'clock curfew, so we were just fiddling around until I kicked him out so I could get some sleep. I was upstairs, he was downstairs, so off he went and I had barely drifted off when all of a sudden comes this tremendous shriek and everyone jumped out of bed and came out of their rooms to see who was being murdered, that's what it sounded like.

Mr. Barth came running out of his apartment at the end of the hall, and went dashing down to the bottom floor where the screaming was coming from. Most of the boys were too scared to venture further than their doorways, but I had a feeling and followed Barth down.

It's hard to describe the scene, in a way, because Lamb's screaming was so loud and terrifying it was hard to actually take in what I was seeing. He was crouched on the floor in the hallway, doubled over in a fetal position, rocking and shaking. His hands were over his ears, and he was screaming and crying like I have never heard anyone in my life. Even when Barth ran to him and tried to calm him, he wouldn't stop—everyone said later that he suffered a psychotic break, or at the very least a nervous breakdown. This went on and on for I don't know how long until another one of the dorm masters arrived on the scene to investigate, and the reason for Lamb's fit was discovered.

At the bottom of his bed, "someone" had taken the fetus pickled in formaldehyde from the biology lab and poured the slimy, shrunken thing under the covers so that Lamb had probably gotten into bed and felt it with his feet, only discovering what it was once he'd jumped out and pulled the sheets back—at least, this is what the dean of students told me they think happened after Thomas was questioned, confessed, and suspended. Apparently *baby* was the message he was trying to convey for snitching on him. They took Lamb off to the infirmary that night, and the next day his mom drove up from LA and withdrew him from school.

We were so close to graduation that I guess they just decided to give him a final grade based on what he had earned already so it wouldn't affect his college prospects. He is listed as part of the graduating class, and he did receive a diploma, though he wasn't at the ceremony, obviously. When Thomas got back from his suspension, he was decidedly cowed and couldn't look me in the eye for the rest of the year.

I had really hoped Lamb would also maybe go to USC

so we could still hang out, but I suspect his mom convinced him to go to Berkeley after all that, and not just because it was a better school. She hadn't yet married her new husband, and half the tuition for private schools was killing her. Also because all our drinking and smoking cigarettes and weed came out while Lamb was being treated for his breakdown, he told me at some point that she thought I was a bad influence.

THE FIRE ROAD PART III

You've moved all your stuff back home. It's understood you won't be boarding anymore. You are a day student again, shuffling up to school for classes and then straight back home. You get closer after that, you and Matt. He is practically living down at your house on the weekends. He spends the night every Saturday and Sunday. Your mom had a word with the dean. Matt's mom gave permission because it's technically not on campus. He says she drinks too much since his brother's accident and has just given up.

Your mom moves one of the single beds from the guest room into your room. There is really only one place to fit it in, right next to yours. They are side by side even though there are separate sheets and blankets.

It happens quick. One Saturday night you stay up late drinking a bottle of wine you stole from your parents' wine cellar. There is a crate of the cheap stuff left over from a school function they hosted. You are feeling toasty. Matt is always complaining about how hot your room is. He opens windows and strips down to his boxers to sleep. You are just dozing off when you feel a rumble. You start awake. You cry out thinking it's an earthquake. Matt laughs softly in the dark.

"I keep falling through the crack between the beds," he says. He's pushed them together.

He whispers in the dark about a party he'd been to last summer. How it had turned into an orgy—they'd all taken ecstasy and were laying together close on lounge chairs around the pool late at night. It was boys and girls, and girls and girls, and boys and boys. You drift to sleep with the soft lull of his words, the warmth of his body and breath beside you. Later you wake up again. His arm is slung over your chest. You can smell the cheap, sweet wine on his breath. His erection is pressed against your hip.

You've been thinking about this for a while. He is handsome like James Dean. He has that darkness about him. Even when all the other guys wear board shorts and flip flops, Matt is always in a white t-shirt and jeans. Feeling him pressed up against you in bed is the most exciting thing that's ever happened to you.

You realize he stripped off his boxers. He is naked. You are only wearing your underwear. You gently squirm your hand down between you and take hold of him. He gasps. He is only pretending to be asleep. You barely stroke it for a few moments. He groans. It bucks and squirts on your hand. He is still pretending to be asleep. You pull tissues from your nightstand and clean up while he lies there. His heavy breaths slowly calm, turn to soft snores.

That's how you end up sleeping in the same bed every weekend. In the mornings you shove the mattresses apart a few inches to preserve the illusion that you are not in bed together. But you are.

There was a reshuffling of classes after winter break. Students sometimes pick up a new elective, and have to switch from one English or history section to another. Somehow in the new year, you ended up with no classes in common with either Matt or Thomas. Although Matt is coming up to your house after class on Saturday and staying until Monday morning, you don't see him much during the week.

Matt decides to go for the tennis team. It turns out he is really good. His dad has a tennis court at his house down in Brentwood. He took private lessons last summer before he came to Wolcott. You see him practicing with the rest of the tennis team on the courts next to the swimming pool, including Thomas. Thomas is ranked number three in the state, or so he says. Only one or two of the other players give him any competition at all. Matt is one of them. One weekend, he mentions what a bunch of pussies most of the players are.

"So, you spend most of your practices playing against him?" you ask.

"Not all—since you tend to play better against a better player, everyone wants a chance to play up to his level." He tries to pass it off as no big deal. It's clear he doesn't want to talk about Thomas anymore, not even to badmouth him.

Your overnights continue through most of the spring. After Easter break, Matt starts making excuses for why he can't spend the weekends at your house. Not every weekend, sometimes just one night, or, coincidentally, on weekends Thomas goes home. You still mess around, but you can't show anything on the outside around your parents or Brett or other people. Even when you are naked in the dark, you hold back.

He wants to go further. One time he crawls on top of your back and starts to push himself inside you. It hurts so bad you yelp. He stops. You don't know how to say *slower* or *gentler*. Words aren't easy. You go back to hands, and you let him suck you but you can't wrap your head around doing the same thing for him. He doesn't ask.

One weekend when he is over, he says he's been home to his mom's in town. She lives right on the beach in one of those big cottages with sand for a backyard. He's gotten ecstasy for you. He's done it before, but you've only ever smoked weed with him a couple times. You are really nervous. Your parents are home. You're worried you'll lose control. They'll hear or start asking questions about why you're acting so strange. Matt says no, it isn't like that. He takes his, but you only take half of your tablet.

He becomes soft and sweet as you start to feel it. He isn't saying anything, but he wants you to hold him tight. He starts to kiss you. You've never done that before. You feel warm and squishy. Before you know it, you are naked. He straddles you. You're inside him. He's bouncing on top of you and stroking himself. You both come. When he rolls off, he leaves a bit of a mess on you and can't stop laughing about it as you're cleaning up.

You've been sneaking down to the pump house to smoke

when your parents are home. One day Matt pulls a glossy magazine out of his backpack and tosses it to you. On the cover in blocky yellow letters, the title "HAMMER." A picture of a man with a chain around his neck and a boot between his shoulder blades holding him down on a cement floor. You puff nervously on your cigarette.

"What's this?" Matt doesn't respond, just smirks. You open to the first few pages and a raw jolt courses through you. There are naked men tied up to chain link fences. In garages and basements. One man's head is completely covered in a leather hood with no eyes and a zipper for a mouth, just two little holes for nostrils so he can breathe. Another is locked in a cell that looks like a jail. His arms are handcuffed behind his back. Another guy, twenty at most, crouches at the foot of a huge hairy older man with a mustache. Leather, sunglasses, cigar, astride his bike. The young man licks the older one's boot.

Matt's eyes are burning with excitement. "Are you into this?" you ask.

"Just read it—read the story on page eighteen." He leans on the iron railing.

You finish your cigarette and turn to page eighteen. "The Trench." It says *Fiction*.

It tells the story of two men seeking revenge on a third who escaped justice for the violent assault and maiming of a friend. The friend was walking home alone one night from the bars. He was accosted on a shortcut through an alley by the perpetrator and another man. The author describes *curbing*: their friend's jaw was lodged on the edge of a curb, and then stomped, breaking teeth and jaw. The other man was never identified, but they know the guy who curbed their friend, a local redneck, handsome and arrogant. They both loathe and lust for him.

The two men have an old, out of business car repair shop in a derelict warehouse district. There is a trench in the floor where the mechanics work on the cars from beneath. They are lovers. They use this place to act out fantasies.

You stop reading. "This is freaky." Matt is wandering around the pump house, examining the padlock, knocking on the gigantic steel pipes. All the water for the campus and the avocado orchards is pumped uphill through them. Matt kicks tentatively at the two-inch nuts securing the joints of the pipes.

"Keep reading, it gets interesting."

The buddies with the trench spend weeks preparing for the captivity of the villain. Steel eye bolts are installed. Thick chains are measured and secured. A drain in the bottom of the trench is cleaned and cleared. A thick black hose with a powerful nozzle is attached to a new spigot on a nearby wall, installed by a gay plumber who is in on the plot. Windows are blacked out. A number of others are included, a group project, the more the merrier. When the time comes, they kidnap the redneck in a van.

While still unconscious, the victim is stripped naked, gagged, and chained by the neck in the trench. He will be spending the next two to three months in there. He must be guarded 24/7. They have to be careful. Someone may notice the comings and goings of a group of eight men. They all wear masks.

The redneck is placed in a stock so he can't move his head. One guy is trained in electrolysis. In painful two and three hour sessions for weeks, he sets about the permanent removal of the guy's thick, luxurious hair, his eyebrows, half of his beard and mustache.

The vigilantes rape him every day. The trench is their toilet. When the smell gets too bad or they want to work on him, they turn the hose on and blast him with cold water. They wake him at regular intervals with the hose until he sobs in exhaustion. One of their members is a tattoo artist by trade. He tattoos the redneck's scalp, face, neck and hands with swastikas, crude penises, the words *FAGGOT, COCKSUCKER, SHITEATER*. They pull out some of his teeth.

Feeding time. At first, he refuses to eat. The guy with medical training inserts a feeding tube through his nose down to his stomach for the first several days until the dude decides it's better to just swallow what is fed to him. They pump him full of super weight-gain formulas mixed from a powder, the kind used by bodybuilders. They fill him with as many calories as he can hold until his stomach gets big and round. Within a month, he gains thirty pounds. In the second month, another twenty. He has great livid stretch marks on his arms, belly, and thighs.

Finally, they drag him out of the trench, and dump him naked in a parking lot. He lives, but he is damaged.

When you finish the story, you are anxious. You say, "So what?"

Matt shrugs, takes back the magazine. "Just think about it."

Right before Memorial Day weekend, the culprit is identified. Matt and Thomas went to the dean. They both saw Burke coming from the vicinity of the dining hall by himself "looking sketchy" that day. Thomas said he saw Burke lurking in the kitchen at the end of breakfast, and that he had a free period that morning when everyone else was already off to class. They hadn't put two and two together before because no one found out what happened until they got back from Christmas vacation. Matt admits to you he's been talking to Thomas about it. He says he's been trying to get Thomas to admit he threw the egg. In the end, they realized it was only Burke who had the opportunity.

Burke doesn't get suspended just on suspicion of having injured you. There are other reasons. His grades are terrible. He's been flunking history since Mr. Stalling left and the new teacher took over. There's been some thievery around the dorm. Matt says his camera went missing. When he told the dorm master about it, they questioned a couple of boys who had been accused of other incidents. Burke's room was searched, and the camera was found hidden in his trunk.

"He denied everything, of course," Matt tells you, "and it was his dishonesty that made them decide he needed to be separated from the school. He might not be asked back next year."

"So, you and Thomas…" You can't look him in the eye. He hasn't been over to your house in a couple of weeks, not since he showed you the magazine. You have the feeling he is trying to distance himself. You haven't been much of an ally hiding out at home while the rest of campus life goes on without you. It's not like you are boyfriends or anything. He says he's just pretending to be friendly with

Thomas to get to the bottom of things.

He's going down to his dad's for Memorial Day weekend, and school is done two weeks after that. He says he is staying at his mom's down in town for most of the summer. He got his provisional license so he can drive up to see you. You feel very unsure of him.

Right after classes the weekend before commencement, they are loading up the buses for the class trips. Sophomores were going up to Yosemite, without you. You've been having trouble with your eye again. An infection has returned that they are treating with strong antibiotics that make you nauseous. You are walking home from the library. As you pass the parking lot with all the guys milling around the buses with their bags, you hear that familiar moaning wail behind you.

"Markensteiiiin...." It's been awhile since you've heard the monster's taunt. It hits you in the gut. You should ignore it, but for some reason, something about the voice makes you turn. And there is Matt, standing next to Thomas, Andrews and Moore, staring right at you. His face is blank. The rest of them are doubled over with laughter, slapping him on the shoulder. You know it was him. So what you'd worried about all these weeks is true. His betrayal is complete.

You just want the last week of school to be over. You've been talking to your parents about transferring to another school though the deadline for applications is long past. Still, no school in the country will refuse the son of Elanor Wolcott, especially since your grades are good. You've considered going down to the local public high school, but nothing is decided.

You are avoiding Matt. Between the taunting and the trip to the pump house, you wonder if he was trying to scare you. Maybe he drank Thomas's Kool-Aid. Maybe he's trying to get in your head. You wonder if he's worried you will out him. You think it's best to let the clock run out on the year.

At morning assembly, Mr. Dennis the classics teacher asks the boys going on his Odyssey summer trip to stay behind. This is an organized sailing expedition the school does every year. Students in his class study the Odyssey and plays by Euripides for their English requirement, instead of reading stuff like Shakespeare and *The Great Gatsby*. They learn a little Greek. They fly off to Athens the day after commencement for an eight-week chartered yacht tour of locations in Homer's Odyssey. Thomas is among them. And so is Matt. Your heart sinks to see them yucking it up together.

It's pretty clear Matt's chosen his side. You can't bear to think about all the time you spent together earlier in the spring. It makes you a little sick to think of it—not so much what you did together, but just how stupid you were to trust him.

He corners you in the library on the last day of classes. You have a free period, and then Mr. Turner's physics team will set off all their homemade rockets on the soccer field for the whole school to watch. You're killing time in your usual cubicle in the back of the upstairs stacks, and Matt sidles up.

"I know what you're thinking," he says, "but I have a plan."

You just stare at him. You surprise yourself. You'd been very timid with Thomas and his gang, but with Matt you feel a righteous sense of betrayal.

He goes on. "I can't tell you what it is. You believe that I'm just playing Thomas, right?"

"That's not what it looks like."

"I know—it can't look like I'm not sincere or he'll know that I'm up to something. But he's going to learn his lesson. What I really want to say is..." He hesitates. "Well. It's funny—I can't really say it out loud now." He clears his throat. You see the gears turning. "So. What if we went on a trip down to Baja together a little later in the summer?"

You can't believe your ears.

"My dad's got this friend who lives down there, he and his girlfriend live in this palapa on the beach and they fish every day, and sell it to the ladies at the fish market in town, and smoke dope and drink beer and live this super peaceful life. I just thought we could go stay down there with them for a while and chill out. Just you and me."

You stand up and gather your books. "You're..." You stop yourself. He might actually be crazy. "We're not doing this." You push past him and head toward the stairs.

Behind you, he says very quietly, "You'll see."

Commencement goes off without a hitch. The senior class has been nice to you for the most part, but you still decide to skip it and stay home. Your parents go, of course, as a trustee Elanor is expected. They come back from the ceremony that afternoon looking flushed and happy. You feel disconnected. You feel like you failed at Wolcott, even though it wasn't your fault.

You don't say goodbye to Matt. You put him out of your mind. No second chances after the games he's been playing. It's a moot point anyway. You've told your mom you're done. She's already made some calls. It looks like you'll have your pick of schools. She'll take you on a trip to visit the two or three most promising ones later in the month.

It's unusually warm. They've been saying it's likely to be a bad fire season. There's been little rain all winter. Your dad's been complaining about the irrigation system. The pump at the reservoir is on the fritz. He lost the key to the pump house, and tore the tool shed apart looking for the bolt cutters. That was two weeks ago. You assume he's taken care of it.

One evening Matt appears out of the blue at your window, shimmies up the trellis and calls to you. Your heart jumps into your throat. You assumed he'd left on the Odyssey trip.

"Listen, I told you I was going to fix this shit with Thomas for you."

He is deadly serious. He has a feverish look about him, like he's been running a marathon.

"Fuck Thomas."

"You can if you want," he says. That's the moment you know something is seriously off. "Come with me."

"Where?"

He insists. Tries to soothe you. Almost pleads. This is important to him. "It's OK, really—Thomas has something to say to you."

"What are you talking about? Thomas is on the trip— you're supposed to be, too. What the fuck is going on?"

"We didn't go." You say that's obvious. "You still want to head down to Baja?" You never said you would. "Listen, just come with me—I want you to see something, and everything will make sense. Please." He steps into your room and comes to you. He grabs you around the waist, but your flesh shrinks from him. You shrug him off.

"How do I know you're not trying to trick me? With all that Markenstein shit, and hanging out with Thomas."

"I promise you everything I did was to trick him into thinking that I was done with you, and that I wanted to be friends with him. He's a dupe. He's the one who actually tried to convince me to stop hanging out with you and be his friend instead. He said I was the only one who isn't afraid of him. And now he wants to apologize."

At this point, you get the feeling you'd better go with him. You have a strong sense suddenly that you aren't the one in danger. Something is definitely wrong. You go out the window with him, and cut out the back of the house down the trail to the big pump house. You keep him talking. He is chattering on about Baja. You only interrupt to say it sounds like fun.

When you get there, there's a shiny new padlock on the door. He pulls the key out of his pocket and stops.

"Don't freak out. He's not going to get hurt if he just does the right thing." The hair on your head stands up. He unlocks the door. It's dark inside. You hesitate. He goes in, and turns on the light. Thomas is lying on the floor.

"Oh my god."

Your mind reels. Thomas looks drugged. His eyes don't focus. He is awake but staring into space. He is dirty. Only wearing his underwear. There is a bucket next to him, and in the far corner a pile of tubing and containers and other things. Your dad's bolt cutters.

Thomas's hand is chained and padlocked to one of the big steel pipes. Also handcuffed. There is no getting out. He looks like a scared little boy.

"What did you do!"

Matt is grim. "Well let's just say he's not a virgin anymore."

"What—"

"Don't worry, he's so full of my mom's Valium, he's feeling no pain." He is pleased with himself. He feels powerful. "You could have a whack at him if you want, and then it's feeding time. He's on a weight gain diet, just like in that story—he should put on about thirty, forty pounds over the next month or so. That's how I'm feeding him the Valium. I'm not starving him or anything."

You've made a mistake coming here. All you can think to do is run out of there and get help. He might try to stop you.

You say, "Let's go outside and talk." He follows you out and leans on the railing along the cliff's edge. He lights a cigarette. He is exultant.

"How...?" You can't finish the question.

"School thinks he had a family emergency and had to pull out of the trip at the last minute. I just said I wasn't going if he wasn't. He thought we were heading down to Baja for the summer, but of course that's not happening, at least not with him. I've got the money my dad gave me for my trip, and the money he brought—we're set. You and me—we can do this. Make him pay, and then disappear into Mexico. Fuck this place, fuck all of them."

"How did you get him in here?"

"He thought we were stocking up for the trip with ecstasy and coke. I told him we could meet my dealer down at the fire road after commencement. I just slipped him a roofie with some vodka and orange juice. He was on the ground in twenty minutes."

You shake your head. "You're going to get caught, you know that." You start to make excuses. You have to think about it. You're not sure.

He knows you're not buying it. He's lost you. He curses, and mumbles something. He pushes past you back to the pump house. He returns with a glass bottle full of a yellow liquid and a rag sticking out of the top.

"Now you're not going to do something stupid are you?" he says. "I did all this for you, Mark. You have to know that. Because ... well, just because, OK? Please..." He's lost his nerve at the last moment. He wants to tell you he loves you, you can feel it. But he knows it's over. You will try to talk him out of whatever this is. You try to reason with him.

"Come with me," you say. "Just put it down and we'll walk out of here, and ... and we'll go to Baja, just like you wanted. But let's leave Thomas out of this—he's a dick, but he's not worth it." He says nothing for a long moment, stares down into the canyon. He's balanced on the top of the railing, one hand holding the bottle.

He lights a fresh cigarette clenched between his teeth, and then he calmly touches the lighter to the rag in the top of the bottle. It catches and burns. He salutes you. You take a step back. Maybe he's going to throw it at you. Instead, he tosses it at the side of the pump house.

You scream and jump back further from the explosion

of gas and flames. When you look back at the railing, Matt is gone.

In a rush, you run around to the pump house door. The walls are cinder block, but the roof is already curling flames and smoke under the eaves. You grab the bolt cutters and cut the handcuff and the chain off of Thomas. You pick him up and drag him out of there. The fire has spread to the shrubs and trees over the path back toward school. You hitch Thomas's arm over your shoulders, walk him down the dirt trail along the side of campus, and then the rest of the way down to the fire road at the bottom of the canyon. At one point you slip. As you are going down your hand lands on a sharp stick. You scream. The skin on the back of your hand is raised. The stick went straight through and tented it. You cry out again as you yank it out.

The whole top of the hill above you is already engulfed. Thomas is useless, clutching you. You will go pound on Penny's door in her cottage at the bottom of the hill. As you stumble down the road in that direction, you see her and her husband already standing out in the road. Fire trucks are blaring sirens and horns. A big one is charging toward you. It stops not fifteen feet away. The headlights are blinding. Thomas hangs off of you, your blood splashed across his bare skin.

THE ECHO OF EMBRACE

I'm not much of a poetry man, but of the hundred or so poems Lamb wrote in his journals—none of them published—this one stood out for me. The title caught my eye, for one thing, because I always thought it was weird that when he saw either of his parents, they didn't hug him. It was like his mom was always mid-thought whenever she arrived, like "Did you remember such-and-such?" or "Hurry up and get in, I've got an appointment at four o'clock." She was also always smoking—which is a hoot considering she thought *I* was the bad influence—so she was always fiddling with her lighter, her purse, cigarettes, keys, too busy fussing to take a moment to give her kid a hug.

His dad, on the other hand, I don't know—he was a diplomat, sort of a big wig at the UN or EU, a fixer behind the scenes rather than someone who would be an ambassador and all that—so in his suits and ties (pretty sure I never saw him in anything else) he always had this air of mild disdain for Lamb and his crazy clothes and hairstyles. If you can imagine a father who wanted to pretend like he didn't know his own son, well, that was pretty much the size of it. Anyway, every time I ever saw them together, his father shook Lamb's hand like he was meeting him for the first time in a boardroom.

When I saw this title and read this poem, I was struck by how Lamb was cast adrift after his parents got divorced—almost as though he got divorced too, which I think is a feeling a lot of people don't want to acknowledge about children when the parents split up. It's one thing to walk away from a bad marriage, it's another to be thrust out into the world too young.

So it's another prose poem, my friend Lawrence tells me—and he really is a poet when he's not running an after-school program for kids in Oakland. I asked him to read through some of them just to see, and he also was struck by this one in particular.

"They're OK, but this one made me think. He's on the edge of saying some really interesting things, but something goes wrong. Was this guy adopted?" he asked me.

"No, but his parents got divorced and sent him to boarding school when he was relatively young."

"That makes sense," he said.

The Echo of Embrace

Willam Broeder

Arms around you, arms drop away. There is no staff so strong, no pillar that does not falter. Endless hope is not the thing itself, never wanted, never was. Can't reach, can't grasp, stretch and strain—a mountain plumbed deep into the earth, rootveins beneath the surface, hidden but sure, a crown so high you can never touch, always just out of sight.

He will never disappoint, keeper of promises, hands never let go. His touch soft as linen and feather, sweetwine and cinnamon breath, wrapped in heat. He holds you, he hopes you, two bodies, no space, no doubt. Two become one, entwined—roots and earth, fire and air. Beeswax candles and new shoots, lemonyellow, glistening green jars and bowls and silvercertainty. Pulsing heartbeats in the womb of quiet night, the red darkness, murmur murmuring.

A fathomless hole, an empty, round spiraling shell, echoing with ancient winds. A round tongue holds you, pushes you out of dreams, pulling you from the depths of sleep into stark wakefulness. Silence breaks into sharp clarity, light cuts through the dark. The enfolding you seek—the touch, the warmth, the shelter—remains elusive, yet you crave it. Everything fleeting, she no different, her hands, once gentle conduits of time, slipping through your fingers, in and out of her embrace endlessly.

The eternal cycle repeats, bloody red to pale viscous

sunlight, whole into zero into nothingness.

Not knowing the only truth, quiet certainty settles, dust on unused windowsills (despite the bishop and the breadswallowing and the devastationhowl) forever merging, filled and emptied. In the stillness, moments pass, whistling on the wind, lost already. Their grip stiffens, withers, falls away.

Love dies and is made new, over and over—the eternal motherfathermoment fills and empties, fills and empties.

(You wonder if love is real, if it can be trusted. It is not the love of yesterday or tomorrow, those days are none. Only the present, only the nowness at the heart of all things. Emptiness your only companion, not full to bursting but hollow. A scream waits to escape. A wail lodges in your throat. You want release, to dissolve, become glass, water, airblank, silencesmoke. You want to shatter, to flow, to gush outward and inward, through and through and through, until nothing is left.)

Whispers in the night slip away like sand through fingers, grasping at the air. Horror is a refusal, a denial, yet you refuse to let go. You hold on to then, to the memory of arms around you, arms that drop away. The paradox repeats, the endless loop of longing, and losing.

DADDIES

After I got the notice from Wolcott that Lamb had died—
yes, I remember now it was February of 2004—and I had
no luck trying to get in touch with his parents, I decided I
better let his friends know what happened. There were
surprisingly few calls to be made. His disappearing act had
severed ties pretty neatly at The Club, the bar where he
worked, and it had a new owner anyway.

His old roommates were nice, and seemed genuinely
sorry to hear it, but only one showed up to the memorial
gathering I arranged at my house. Lindsey happened to be
coming to town to visit her parents the next weekend. She
was seven months pregnant. We decided to do it on a
Saturday afternoon.

Fugie had a hysterical crying fit on the phone when I
called him, which sounded genuine enough, I suppose, but
I had to draw the line when he started pressing for all sorts
of special rituals he wanted to plan for the gathering. He

wanted me to call Wolcott (again) and get a forwarding address or phone number for Lamb's parents so we could determine the exact day he had died. He was on a Buddhist kick, and planned to invite some monks to chant over an altar he wanted to put together in my house—it was important that it be done on the seventh day—and he wanted everyone to wear white and I don't know what all.

I told him I wasn't chasing down Lamb's parents—and no, I wouldn't give him the number to the Wolcott alumni office so he could do it, fuck sake, I'd already tried. It had definitely been far longer than seven days by that time, probably at least a few months. No random Buddhist monks, thank you, but I did ultimately let him put together a little altar on a table with some pictures, candles, and incense. Of course he went overboard and had about twenty sticks of incense going at one time. I had to put a stop to it and open up all the windows because everyone was choking and he kept shushing us while he was trying to chant.

In the end there were only about ten of us, including Lindsey's mom, Hazel, who had met Lamb a few times and said she always wished Lindsey might have married him. Lindsey didn't entirely disagree, but she was no dummy and had opted to take a sisterly approach with him from the get-go.

We did a little candle pass and said a few words each—three guesses who went on and on for twenty minutes—and then after a toast to his memory, people started to drift out when the whole chanting/incense ridiculousness started, despite Fugie yelling that no one could leave until he'd finished. Finally, I had to push him out the door under the pretense that Lindsey wasn't feeling well and needed to lie down for some peace and quiet. Once everyone else was gone and her mom was in the kitchen washing up, we had a chance to talk for a bit.

"Well, you know, I didn't want to say anything after he took off because it wasn't my business to tell tales," she said. "But now that he's gone, it won't hurt for you to know the truth."

I always thought Lindsey was this incredibly sweet but tough chick, no nonsense, but also she knew how to have fun—she is the one who dragged him up to Burning Man, after all. She was kinda gorgeous with this dark auburn hair and cute little bangs, a smattering of freckles, just a little lipstick-and-go kind of gal. Her mom brought us two mugs of chamomile tea, and we sat on the sofa while she told me what happened during Lamb's last days in San Francisco.

If you spend any amount of time on the party and dating scene in SF, eventually you are going to come face-to-face with someone offering you crystal meth. Cocaine was also big with the restaurant crowd and bartenders. Apparently Lamb had been dabbling with some of his coworkers, and it was just a hop, skip and a jump from coke to crystal, which was generally cheaper and more powerful. Thank god I never got into it. I had a friend early on in our party days that I had a big crush on and lent some money very stupidly, and it turned out he was already caught up in a pretty bad meth addiction and I never saw the money again, or him.

It's always good to have a cautionary tale before you even get going with something like that. I'm sure I told

Lamb about it, and I think it might have warned him off at first, but that might also be why he never talked to me about it once he started using. As I dropped away from partying and started focusing more on my career and normal stuff, Lamb was inching his way down the white brick road. Maybe it's hard to resist when it's front and center all the time.

The Club had a reputation for being edgy—there was a backroom, and always at least one naked guy hanging out on full display—so it attracted a certain element, the PNP (party and play) crowd, which basically means *let's get high as fuck and have freaky sex*. I suppose I should be more surprised that it took so long for Lamb to get sucked into all that than that he did.

According to Lindsey, Lamb was at a low ebb right around the time I left for Austin. He got dumped again, and he'd been depressed when he hooked up with this older couple who had a big house on Potrero Hill. Apparently they were both really good looking, and had successful careers as attorneys, the older one retired, but the younger one still practicing. They took a shine to Lamb and invited him up to their house one night, sort of dazzled him with their sex appeal and glamorous views, and they introduced him to smoking meth, which is even more messed up than crack and sort of the next step if you're into no-holds-barred sex parties.

"Lamb's not my only gay friend who got twisted up in that mess," Lindsey said. "My one friend told me some hair-raising stories after he got clean. He was shooting up by the end, and he still goes to NA meetings every single day."

Weed, alcohol, meth, Special K, and GHB —at least those are the ones Lamb told Lindsey about when she visited him in rehab. I told her I was surprised she let him sublet her place, knowing what was going on, and she said she initially said *no* but that she changed her mind when he mentioned that I was going to share the sublet with him and she knew how responsible I was.

Anyway, she said these guys were really into the Daddy/boy thing, and that they loved the idea of sharing Lamb as their own personal sex toy. They collared him, which is that little chain with a padlock you see around these guys' necks sometimes, and it basically meant he was their property and they could do whatever they wanted with him. They called themselves a throuple, and wanted Lamb to move in with them. They had a full-on dungeon in their basement with the works—St. Andrews cross, restraints, sling, leather, floggers and all that.

Within just a couple months, Lamb was spending all his time with them, and they were having these wild parties with friends coming over with their boys, and slaves too, and some puppies, which are basically these guys who wear dog masks and leather puppy paws and tails which I won't tell you how they wear those. If they misbehaved (usually on purpose) they would get put into the crate as a punishment, this big metal cage, and forced to do humiliating things in order to get out.

And that's where things went really wrong. They'd all been up for two days partying, and at some point Lamb blacked out, and when he woke up, he was locked in the crate in the pitch-black basement alone and he completely freaked out. He started screaming and banging around, like a caged animal obviously, and he made such a ruckus that the neighbors heard and called the cops. By the time the Daddies got him out and calmed down, the police were already at the front door, and only by sheer bravado these two attorneys were able to talk themselves out of a search of their house which would have turned up who knows what kind of drugs and paraphernalia.

Well they were pissed as hell after the cops left, but who could blame poor Lamb for being freaked after what happened to him in high school? They kicked him out, said they needed a boy that could handle himself, and that was that.

But that wasn't that—Lamb was completely strung out, hadn't been to his job in a while, and had been using heavily with them for several months. A few nights later, he got black out drunk and snuck into their house through an unlocked window to steal their drugs. The older one walked in on Lamb rifling through their stash, and a struggle ensued.

I guess the guy thought that because Lamb had been their boy and he had been playing submissive all that time that he could push him around and get him out of the house. But by virtue of six-feet-six inches, two-hundred-fifty-plus pounds, and enough vodka to anesthetize an elephant, Lamb beat him up pretty badly, not really even knowing what he was doing, like three black eyes and a dislocated funny bone—I joke, but it really was serious. So much for playing big bad Daddy to Lamb in a blackout.

It's good that he didn't get away with the drugs because they had a sizable stash that could have landed him in big trouble. As it was, they didn't want to get the police involved and risk more scrutiny on their activities so they let it drop, but gave Lamb a good scare with threats about what would happen if he ever came near them again.

When he finally snapped out of it the next day and pieced together what he had done, it scared the shit out of him. He called his parents and told them he needed help, and they found him an in-patient rehab center up in wine country, which I always thought was totally cockamamie, but they supposedly have a good success rate, all things considered.

TO LAMB

"What do you think it was?" Lindsey asked me as we were drinking our chamomile tea.

Her mom really had started to feel a little ill and went into the bedroom to lie down. Turns out she was in the throes of breast cancer, and only lived long enough to celebrate Lindsey's baby's first birthday—Hazel, they named her after her grandma. The picture Lindsey emailed when her mom died was from baby Hazel's birthday party, and Grandma Hazel looked strangely amazing with this wild blonde wig, like Debbie Harry came for cake and kisses with her grandbaby. Happiness can erase all kinds of troubles, if only for an afternoon.

Lindsey's question smacked me between the eyes because I had been thinking back to a time when Lamb and I were talking about death, not that it was a common thing, but something struck me about what he said.

"It's written somewhere, you know?"

I can still see us kicked back on the hood of my dad's LTD out in the Mojave Desert. We drove straight out of Lancaster until we ran out of road, then turned off onto a dirt track with just a bunch of Joshua trees standing around us like bristling shamans.

That far away from the city, the Milky Way was on full display—Lamb had never seen it before, and he was getting all Cosmic Carl on me. *Star-stuff*, he called us, goggling over the night sky, and how we both had been born in the space age, within weeks of the first man on the moon.

We'd made a bong out of a jelly jar and some plastic tubing, spray painted it gold—we named it *The Golden Gun*—and stayed out there until almost midnight smoking weed, drinking warm beer we stole from my parents' garage, listening to tapes and talking.

Written somewhere, he said, and I asked, "What's written where?"

"What do you think it will be? What will kill us?"

I said I hoped it wasn't a kill situation and more of a dead in the morning sort of thing. "But what do you mean by *written*?"

"Just that a hundred years from now, or however long, our cause of death will be written, and it's a definite thing, you know, like it *is* going to be something, and we just don't know what it is yet, but someday someone will record it, and I'm just wondering what they'll write down?"

"And when," I added.

But that was the conversation I flashed back to when Lindsey asked me how I thought it happened. I hadn't had any luck finding out Lamb's cause of death. I did call

Wolcott, but they had no further information and I didn't even ask if they could get a message to Lamb's mom and dad. I tried to search obituaries, but the internet was still pretty clunky back then.

The big ones: overdose, suicide, AIDS. We rattled them off, sitting there on the sofa, but neither Lindsey or I had the heart to start speculating out loud what it was, and just then, Hazel came out of the bedroom and said she was ready to get going home. We said our goodbyes, and come to think of it, that's the last time I saw them, too, other than the picture Lindsey sent. We're friends on Facebook, but we were never really close like she and Lamb were.

I'm not sure what I thought, honestly, about how Lamb actually died. In a way, the moment he took off without saying goodbye was when he died to me, even though it was a hopeful absence until I got the note from Wolcott. The adjustment to SF without Lamb was harder than I expected. I'd been away for a year—lots of friends were leaving San Francisco in the early aughts, what with the tech boom and rising rents. The energy of the City changed dramatically. Eventually I hit my stride, but just when I started to feel settled, along came *we regret to inform you...*

Are any of the possibilities preferable to the others? For whatever reason, I didn't think it was probably AIDS. We'd kept a fairly routine testing schedule—whenever it was time for me to get tested, whether because of a dick slip or just because a year had gone by and it was a good thing to do, I'd call Lamb and we'd head up to Health Center 1 on 17th Street in the Castro. We'd both always been negative. Even if he did fall into some unsafe shit near the end, I just thought it was unlikely that he would have slipped away so quickly.

Overdose? Of course, that seemed more plausible after Lindsey told me what he'd been up to, but again, it just seemed like a pretty steep dive from smoking meth to shooting up, which is how most of those things happen, or maybe that's just my bias.

I had a hard time imagining Lamb getting into that anyway, he was such a huge baby about blood and guts and needles. HIV testing was bad enough, he'd always come out of the blood draw looking white as a ghost. One time the guy had to prop him up when he almost fainted. He said the room was really quiet and he heard his own blood squirting into the syringe and started to see stars.

The last biggie though, that's what really got to me, because as much as it killed me to think it, I could see all of his troubles coming to a head, and Lamb—lonely, who knows where, strung out—maybe taking a bunch of pills and slipping away quietly because he just couldn't figure out how to move forward, and no way to come back.

I know, now, what happened—sort of—the other most obvious possibility.

The walk down memory lane, after all this time—well, it was good. Good to remember Lamb, good to finally open up all those boxes, smell his grassy smell, read some of our old letters and peek into his journals. I shared some of his poetry with Lawrence, and I think that was OK, but this isn't going to be some kind of Emily Dickinson thing where I'm championing his writing now after he's gone because he was such a great poet or something.

Anyway, it all prompted me to peek around again

online to see if I could find an obituary, and I finally did. June 15, 2003. That was it, just a date, so in the end it was almost eight months afterward that the notice from Wolcott came.

There was a request in the obit for contributions in Lamb's name to a Jewish temple near Bronxville, New York where his dad and stepmom had lived. A few more clicks, and I found a random note that his dad left a few years ago on the temple's message board for a family grieving the loss of a daughter who had died in an auto accident, a friend of the family probably. Mr. Broeder told them that his own son had died the same way.

So. Car crash.

Was he driving drunk? Was it his fault, or someone else's? Did he die instantly? I don't know, and honestly, I don't want to. But also: Lamb was Jewish? Huh. The things you find out after the fact, right?

I don't remember where I was on the day it happened—it was a Sunday, in summer—but I do remember the next day after our little service for Lamb. It was February in 2004, and I went to one of the gay weddings at San Francisco City Hall, officiated by DA Kamala Harris, of all people. It was a new day back then. Not sure where we're headed now.

I kept the note I read during the candle pass, in case anyone is interested. Here's what I said:

Thank you all for coming today—it may be a small group, but I don't think any of us thinks less of Lamb because there's not a whole gang of mourners. He was a very special guy—strange, some thought, even I thought—and different. Gentle. Serious. Ridiculous. He was all of those and so much more.

I think back to the time he cried his eyes out over a little baby chick, and how I said to myself then, jeez, this kid is completely defenseless, all six-foot-six of him.

For some very special people, there's something missing, some essential ingredient, like leavening in bread—without it, you never get any lift. He was always floundering around, making the same mistakes over and over, and yet he was so bright, one of the smartest people I ever met, and it's really hard to understand sometimes how our favorite people fall and never get back up.

Can we be our best selves without knowing some-one like Lamb, someone who can't cope, good through and through, but never tough enough to hack it here in this great blast furnace of humanity? Can we be our best selves without loving someone like that—the chick that never flies, the babe in the woods who never finds his way home?

Sometimes people are lost and never found. And their legacy for us must not be a turning away from the broken, the strange and difficult, but instead a warm fire of the heart to always return to—always another chance to rise.

I know I would have given Lamb another chance. I wish he had known it. I wish he had been able to shed whatever shame and fear he held inside and given himself that chance.

We say goodbye today knowing that he has found

his way. Please join me in raising a glass. May he fly at last. To Lamb.

ABOUT THE AUTHOR

Troy Ford is an author and editor, and the publisher of two prominent newsletters: the writing-focused FORD KNOWS, and Qstack, an LGBTQIA+ Directory, Platform, and Community of newsletter writers and readers. As a creator and advocate, his mission is to give voice to queer people and issues by promoting their visibility through media projects and collaborations, and through his own fiction and essays.

Troy's writing explores the joy and pain of queerness through the lens of gay men who struggle in a world that views their lives as *other* and *less than*. His themes include love and sex, romance and friendships, community and family, growing up and bullying, substance abuse and self-destructiveness—all with a touch of humor to lighten otherwise difficult topics.

A native Californian, he grew up overseas in the Middle East and eventually settled in the San Francisco/Bay Area where he earned a B.A. in Rhetoric from UC Berkeley. Since 2019, he has lived in Sitges, Spain with his husband and AmStaff Terrier.

Subscribe to his newsletter for updates and insights at: www.troyford.substack.com

Printed in Dunstable, United Kingdom